Advance praise for

CORNER OF THE DEAD

"*Corner of the Dead* is keen and passionate—a sexually alive elegy. Lurie's hypnotic language is as subversive as Seuss in its indictment of racism, bullies, and demigods. A stunning debut."—Fran Gordon, author of *Paisley Girl*

"In this haunting, powerful novel, Lynn Lurie explores not only 'the corner of the dead,' but that entire shadowy no-man's-land where the dead and those who remember them—or more accurately, those who cared enough to try to save them—play out the elemental trauma of their shared experience. Lurie's strong, spare prose will stay with you long after the reading; the truths she tells of life and death in one of the hardest places on earth will stay with you even longer."—Ben Fountain, author of *Brief Encounters with Che Guevara: Stories*

"*Corner of the Dead* has the indelible feeling of a dream you can't shake, a terror made beautiful. It moves by sensation, association, with great fluidity and urgency."—Noy Holland, author of *What Begins with Bird: Fictions*

CORNER OF THE DEAD

CORNER
of the DEAD

LYNN LURIE

University of Massachusetts Press
Amherst

Copyright © 2008 by Lynn Lurie
All rights reserved
Printed in the United States of America

LC   2007049777
ISBN 978-1-55849-654-5

Designed by Steve Dyer
Set in Berkeley Book by dix!
Printed and bound by The Maple-Vail Book Manufacturing Group

Library of Congress Cataloging-in-Publication Data

Lurie, Lynn, 1958–
    Corner of the dead / Lynn Lurie.
        p.   cm.
    ISBN 978-1-55849-654-5 (pbk. : alk. paper)
1. Photojournalists—Fiction.   2. Americans—Peru—Fiction.
3. Sendero Luminoso (Guerrilla group)—Fiction.   4. Peru—History—
1980—Fiction.   5. Peru—Politics and government—1980—Fiction.
6. Indians of South America—Peru—Fiction.   7. Indians, Treatment
of—Peru—Fiction.   8. Genocide—Peru—Fiction.   9. Political fiction.
10. Psychological fiction.   I. Title.
    PS3612.U774C67   2008
        813'.6—dc22   2007049777

British Library Cataloguing in Publication data are available.

Greatful acknowledgment is made to the following
for permission to reprint previously published material:

Mark Strand, for "Song" and "War Song" (on pages 56–58 and 41) from
18 Poems from the Quechua (Cambridge, Mass.: H. Ferguson, 1971); excerpt
(on page 10) from *Fire in the Andes* by Carleton Beals (Philadelphia:
J. B. Lippincott, 1934); excerpt (on pages 39–40) from *One Hundred Years of
Solitude* by Gabriel García Márquez, English translation © 1970 by Harper
and Row Publishers, Inc., by permission of HarperCollins/Avon; excerpts
from "Algo Te Identifica . . . / Something Identifies You . . ." and "Los Nueve
Monstruos / The Nine Monsters" (on pages 106–7 and 134) from *The
Complete Poetry: A Bilingual Edition* by César Vallejo, © 2007 by University
of California Press, by permission of the publisher.

For Barnett and Franny;
and Ruby in memory

El mundo se oscureció
y el agua se secó

The world went black
and the water dried up

> *"Blanca Viente Años Despúes"*
> *"Blanca Twenty-five Years Later,"*
> *2005*

Part I

CHAPTER 1

THERE ARE PLACES in the Andes where we are afraid of dust. Of what might be borne in the dust. We crossed the border and two men in camouflage stepped out from a shack with a corrugated roof, machine guns strapped like mail bags across their chests. They stopped each car and told the passengers to get out.

An Indian boy with a hose attached to a plastic tank worn on his back like a knapsack—it's called a *bomba*—sprayed the inside of the car, then the outside, focusing on the tires. He wore no shoes, no gloves, no mask. The last blast was at eye level. I coughed. As I caught my breath tears ran down my cheeks.

Where we waited densely planted fields lined the highway, wound through hills connected by footpaths, and that is where I saw them, so many women dressed in brilliant colored skirts, ribbons braided through their hair, babies strapped to their backs, stooped over the earth, never standing upright, dropping bean after bean into sisal sacks they dragged behind them.

I took their photographs and they smiled for me. A baby's urine ran down one woman's back and pooled in the dust before being swallowed by the earth.

If bugs and fungus attack a field a village's livelihood can be destroyed. But bugs and fungus don't know about borders made and remade by men across history. I don't remember the men asking for passports and they didn't check for arms. They were worried about the dust, even though there was a war going on in the countryside.

As we pulled away we knew there was no longer anything living in the dust that rose from the underbody of the car. What we didn't know was that in the ravines and ditches along this part of the Pan American Highway, mass graves had been dug and covered, that this earth held the bodies of the disappeared.

If I hadn't been preoccupied with the pesticides I might have thought the freshly tilled soil meant something more than beans and corn being planted and harvested.

Had I known the half-life of the pesticide's poison, I might have stood on the side of the road and waited for the air inside the car to clear, and maybe then I would have seen something.

Inside the car I pulled my T-shirt over my nose. I imagined the insecticide particles sticking to my moist and healthy lungs, taking hold there, duplicating. My repeated coughing did not allay my worry. The man I was traveling with was annoyed at me for being self-absorbed.

When I learned what was in the freshly tilled earth I knew he had been right.

The man beside me on the flight aims an aerosol can and sprays it in front of him. It's not an anti-bacterial so it's not the flu or SARS he's afraid of. He's afraid, I think, of the smell, but there is no smell, just airplane smell and not even stale airplane smell. It is the dust again.

It rises from my blanket as I pull it closer to my face. It

drifts, floats, but doesn't land. Maybe this is what he's afraid of. I don't ask. I want to believe we have something in common.

When I was little, I followed the flecks of dust that my grandmother sent into orbit each night when she pulled the curtains. Some fell on my flannel comforter and merged with the wallpaper's repeating pattern of the shepherd boy playing a bugle on the mountainside. I asked my grandmother what all those dots were. With authority she said she saw nothing. Even when I pointed them out.

I have a small box of dust I shook from my sweater. It fell from my hair and scalp late Tuesday afternoon. It had been there since the morning. I threw my head forward across the dresser surface and used my fingers to shake it from my hair. But there was more, it kept coming.

My daughter's TV was on. The note on the kitchen table said young children should be kept away from the TV. I ran my hand across her things when I first came in, the pencil holder shaped like a fish, glitter pens and multicolored papers. There would be no school tomorrow. How would Thursday differ from Wednesday?

My son came into my room. I asked if his school had let out early. He shook his head yes then cupped the dust on my dresser between his hands. I told him to get the trash can. He swept all of it into my wooden box.

I should turn the box over to the authorities. My neighbor's ashes might be in it. But my son won't part with it.

I AM STARING at the toast on my plate. The lightly browned texture reminds me of freckles. I carve a mouth by cutting a section from the middle, curve the empty space upwards to make a smile. After slicing two eyes I say out loud, Lulu is who you are, Lulu. Now I cannot eat her. The woman beside me moves away, taking her coffee, napkin and silverware.

That was yesterday. I was on my way to work but never got there. It started after I dropped my daughter at school. I felt I was falling, that I could not stop but also could not land. This was when I pulled to the side of the road to see if I could put myself into some sort of order. I called the doctor.

Meet me at the hospital at noon, she said. Sign in as a day patient.

I imagine the hospital, a brick box with two small windows and many missing roof tiles. On the top floor, underneath a no-shingle part, the linoleum will be covered with rust-colored stains. Then I see it, a discolored mushroom rising from black tarry mud.

Each day is like the one before.
Slowly they introduce minute changes.

To teach us to manage uncertainty.

I walk, but not to any one place and not for exercise. Up and around the hallway shaped like a box. When I have completed five boxes I spend as long as they let me just sitting.

Beyond the grimy window, past the driveway across the highway, regular people are having lunch. A coworker is in line at the post office and the woman in the office next to mine makes a call home.

I'm not hungry.

Still I'm required to sit in the cafeteria with the others.

The woman in the hairnet asks, what will it be?

I pick based on color. Today it's yellow. A hardboiled egg, butter and marmalade. In front of me is my plate of food. I move it around making designs.

The way I conserve calories is to sit very still in front of the television but only if it is off. When they turn it on, I move my chair closer to the ping pong table. Then I shut my eyes and concentrate on the sound of the ball as it pings back and forth like the rain, the way I remember it sounding, in Perú. I am thinking I should not have gone back, not after what I saw the first time, but it was in the returning that I thought I could undo what had been done. So little had changed.

Arye never left.

Karl stayed until the end.

I left midway.

I am a coward.

The rain seeped through our roof and dripped into the zig-zag of pots we lined in a row.

Karl says, your turn to empty.

It has been twenty years since I have heard Karl's voice but I haven't forgotten it, or his posture, the way I would see him from our bedroom window, bent over the soil, pieces of corn husk caught in the weave of his poncho. It is the end of the day and the air smells of burning eucalyptus, of fire and ash.

I want to ask the doctors why the pain of remembering has not subsided. Outside the main office is a plaque that says this building was once a school. With my legs crossed and my eyes closed, I am able to imagine the children running through the corridors, their starched and ironed shirts untucked.

When the doctors aren't looking, I run my left hand along the back of my neck checking for cerebral fluid. I have never found any, which keeps me wondering how it might feel and what color it would be.

Blue? But then it would be difficult to look at the sky.

Garbage bins are aligned outside the window. Strewn on the ground are handwritten pages, empty pill containers, a torn hospital gown and a pink plastic tray from the dining hall. The handwritten pages in red ink spell the words that made the sentences scrawled on the stone walls outside our village. The crushed pill bottles are the remains of blown-up dynamite. The torn hospital gown belongs to an Indian girl, the one floating in the muddy river. I only saw part of her. At first I hoped it was the torso of a doll but there were no dolls there. That pink plastic dining tray is holding something, the insides of a pig?

No, that was what they did to the dogs.

I get up abruptly.

The bathroom is the only room with a mirror. I spend a lot of time washing my hands and then I study myself. If someone is next to me, I study the someone else. They should take the mirror down. All I need is one shoe with a heel—and I have two—in order to shatter the whole thing.

I don't know if my chart says I am violent. What they write goes unchallenged. I begin by counting the cracks in the whites of my eyes because I prefer not to look at my face. These blood-red lines are like the tiny veins on the ceramic teacup in yester-day's coffee shop, the one that came with Lulu.

Because I have given a lot of thought to going blind I reassure myself it is a good thing I am seeing all this detail. Once, I tried to stop seeing detail. In Ayacucho, blindness was something that came to me if I was desperate and lucky at the same time. It wasn't just using the camera to block my view, it was a migraine-like blindness and when it came I was able to perfect my hearing. This made me think if I had to, I could manage blindness.

How many cracks more before the cup crumbles into shiny porcelain dust? I should finish counting today because tomorrow I might not see this well. When I make myself finish I lean against the wall. Exhausted. And try to dream. In my daydreams I look for Arye. That was the beginning. I should start with the beginning but I don't want to tell the doctors about Arye. He was in my Quechua class the summer after the Iranians took U.S. hostages. The United States government offered scholarships for the study of sensitive languages. It was an easy commute on Monday to New Haven and back to New York on Friday. The winter following the class, he called. The first snow was falling. Winter is my favorite season. There is a way to travel from winter to winter by crossing the equator. While we were on the phone I made a trough by running my finger through the inch of fine dust that had collected on the sill. I traced the cracks in the granite, then drew a skyline that looked like New York's.

He might have heard the fire engine's siren. He was explaining that the violence in the highlands had escalated. Llacchua, Ataccara, Yanacollpa, Huaychao and Lucanamarca. Then, these were only the names of cities on the map of Perú. The traffic light flashed on Broadway, from green to yellow to red.

· · ·

We arrived a day before the first site visit was sched-
uled. A line in the book I read on the plane said, "Ayacucho
seems more closely linked with death than life. Revolutions
start in Arequipa, says the Peruvian adage. When they reach
Ayacucho, the matter is serious."

CHAPTER 3

SILENCE is reserved for churches.

It should not apply to cities.

Nor steal the voices of children and their animals.

Outside the hotel window the streets of Ayacucho were frozen like those in a travel poster. I strained for the sound of an Indian harp. All I heard were gunshots. I tried to convince myself it was the sound of a muffler backfiring.

Rolff was the first person to introduce himself. I waited for the rest of his name. He only said Rolff. He was a doctor from Germany. As the weeks went on Rolff's expression never changed.

Francisco sat next to him and fidgeted with a knife. I stared past his hands into the alleyway outside the hotel window. Even though the curtain was nearly drawn, I could see *Viva la Guerra* written in red across planks of wood haphazardly nailed into the front of what was once a building. Now it was mostly rubble that could not be held back; chunks of cement were strewn on the walkway and had spilled into the street.

Marta sat next to Francisco. She was from Lima. The wine did not relax her.

Except for the time when missionaries sent Pablo and his

brother to school, he lived where he was born, in an Indian village north of Ayacucho. His brother had gone on to study at the University of Ayacucho. This was where his brother met Shining Path's leader. They hadn't heard from him since. Pablo speculated once he joined *Sendero* it would have been difficult for him to leave. He guessed he had tried because he could not imagine his brother threatening other Indians to plant their land for *Sendero*. The ideas of justice and change, he could see, but the other part, having to prove he was capable of violence, no.

It would had to have been true, Pablo said, or else his brother would not have lasted. Then Pablo paused. I think he was seeing his brother as not having lasted.

The bulge beneath his dark blue poncho must have been a gun.

Before dinner was served and after introductions were made, we sat together but did not speak.

The cook's children played in the courtyard adjacent to the dining room window. It was enclosed by an ancient stone wall. Green moss was growing on the inside, the part that was in shadow. The cook tapped frequently on the glass, motioning to her children to stay within view.

Dinner was soup of yucca, chicken and corn. Yucca is bitter and stringy and difficult to digest.

When we finished, Arye said breakfast would be at five. He pointed to a map with red lines running every which way, each originating in Ayacucho.

I took out my pen and small wire-bound notebook.

Pablo said, distances in the Andes can be deceiving.

I wrote, "camera, film, water," then connected my three-dimensional boxes to other three-dimensional boxes before turning the page and putting the notebook away.

We cleared our places.

Arye continued to study the map.

I could not sleep. It was nearly midnight when I left the hotel. The sky was starless and there was no moon. Hare Krishnas ran a restaurant next door but didn't serve tea steeped in the leaves of the coca plant. The man at the front desk said this was what I needed. I walked to a bar two blocks from the square. The tea helped with the nausea but made me restless.

When the alarm sounded I had just begun to dream.

On the bus I sat next to Marta. She was agitated just like she'd been the night before. I couldn't tell if she had slept, if the cold was bothering her or if she needed coffee. I tried to get her to talk. I wanted to avoid looking outside at the gray day and at the rows of untended corn. But she didn't say anything.

The silence of Ayacucho, that stillness, was echoed in the countryside. Even the wind could not make the fields of barley whistle. It was the kind of cold that comes from damp and is enforced by wind. I was able to see my breath.

Francisco smoked cigarettes, lighting one off the end of the other.

The bus stopped at a place that seemed no different from any other. We got off near a stanchion of eucalyptus trees, the exposed roots clinging to the eroded slopes.

If I had to I could find that place again, exactly.

We climbed for four hours until we reached a village of mud huts. The roofs were thatched eucalyptus and intertwined stalks of barley.

Pablo announced our arrival in Quechua. His voice echoed.

I heard Francisco exhale.

We walked to the center courtyard.

No one.

Pablo asked Arye what to do.

Arye told him to announce we had come to document what was happening in the highlands.

There was no answer, only the rain falling on the dried leaves of the unharvested corn.

Pablo walked inside the first hut.

Rolff fumbled in his shirt pocket for another cigarette. If it weren't for the altitude and the quiet, I would have asked for one. When he found the pack, he stood looking into the silent fog, the cigarette dangling unlit between his fingers.

Pablo called to us.

The fire in the entrance was stone cold. Off to the side was a bale of dried weeds covered by a red blanket. There were three bodies on top of each other. One man's head had been severed and was positioned on the ledge. Had the eyes not been gouged out he would have been looking at us straight on.

There were no flies.

I moved toward the doorway.

I vomited the soup from the night before. It landed between me and Marta.

Rolff was off to the side but could see everything. He glanced up before lighting his cigarette.

Arye held his notebook and tape recorder. I heard him say the date and time in English before pausing the machine. He said to me, you need to photograph this.

I didn't have my camera and I couldn't remember where I'd left my bag.

CHAPTER 4

THERE WERE three more villages that day.

Then a month of villages.

Rolff made lists.

Arye wrote down phone numbers and passed them to Marta.

Marta spent the evenings making calls.

I used the camera to block my view.

We drove by blackened fields, past animals with rigid legs facing upwards. In the distance clothing smoldered in the ditches. There were abandoned houses, singed landscapes, the threat of human remains or no people at all. And in the ground, gaping holes that could have held entire bodies.

Blood, I learned, leaves a film of scum across dust.

The groan of an animal tethered to a post sounded like a child crying. The villagers would have been rushing to grab a poncho or one last thing. A single shoe, a filthy hair tie was all that held their place. I wanted the clothing that had been left out to dry to fill with warm bodies, to see the faces of the people who had lived here, not their remains.

CHAPTER 5

December 13

Freezing cold morning.

Our first stop is a village that took over two hours to reach. We come across an old woman. She isn't moving. I think she must be dead. Then I see her move. I could be imagining this because I am afraid to see a dead person. Her rubber boot sticks out from under a stack of hay.

Pablo moves quickly. He drops his knapsack to the ground. He is on his knees pushing at the stalks. She is not caught but is hiding.

She has gray hair. Most people here don't live long enough to get gray hair. She has many teeth missing.

Her eyes open then shut. Pablo tells us to back away. I want to run but move slowly. I'm walking backwards focused on her rubber boot; one foot has no boot. She may be the oldest woman in what was once a community.

A long time goes by. I'm not sure how long. Time spent waiting is longer than it really is but not long enough, because when it is over the next thing to come is often worse than waiting.

Pablo tells Arye we need to go into the nearest town.

*Arye has the driver take us. We stop in front of an
unfinished courtyard. There are steel rods pointing to the
sky and cinderblocks piled on the side. There are no sounds.
Pablo knocks on the door. He goes inside while we wait
on the bus. When he returns he is carrying dried rice and
beans, water and a blanket.*

*We drive to where we left the woman. She's no longer
there. Pablo stacks the food at the edge of the cornfield,
exactly where her feet had been.*

The wind and the dust, I learned, had been condemned to
carry ashes.

I wanted to say we had been to one village or another; that
we had looked but had found nothing. This, Arye would not
allow.

In our first week Arye bought each of us a shovel. When
he sensed something more than what could be seen, he had
us dig. If there was a place with freshly dug soil or mounds of
packed earth he made us keep going. Sometimes he followed a
handwritten map. Even without the map he was usually right.

On the third day Marta collapsed.

She said it was thirst.

Arye gave her water and walked her to the bus. She slept all
afternoon across the back seat. We kept digging.

The next day she was back at work.

If the repetition began to lull us, something would shock us
back.

I learned not to be lulled.

Even on a clear day, when the mountains shone in the distance, when the glacial streams continued their downward

flow, there was no way to harness the calm. All I let myself see was the dirt beneath my feet. When I had to look up I kept my eyes on the path directly in front of me.

Happy New Year.
That is what the cook said.
Marta wished her the same.
She served the same soup we ate our first night.
We did not discuss the schedule or the route. Breakfast was at 5. We were back by nightfall. Dinner was at 7. The cook prepared lunch for us each morning. We ate it or we didn't around midday.

Arye and I spent New Year's Eve sifting through the photographs, trying to impose some sort of order. I can't look, I finally said. I am seeing more detail now than when we were there.

Arye poured glasses of *chicha*, a local spirit made from potatoes. I stood and faced him. I was about to say I want to go home but sighed instead. If he hadn't been reading and had been watching me I would have said that. I felt ashamed. I turned and pressed my face against the cold window.

I wanted to be home looking out at Riverside Park. To nestle myself in my bed of fresh linen, to feel the heat from the radiator and the noise of all the many people in New York going in and out of the evening.

He took my hand and led me to his single bed. He said, I cannot help you with the loneliness, only with the cold.

That night I heard a cry that was mine. It echoed back a different sound, as though one hundred women were mourning. At 3:47 a.m. I woke him and said, I'm having trouble breathing.

He held onto me.

Neither of us went back to sleep. We watched the shadows that the moonlight made, the way they fell across the wooden dresser and bathed the clothing on the floor.

We held our breath for fear we would break the quiet. Or that we would break.

I wrote this letter later that week.

> *DEAR ARYE:*
> *The clock says 3:47, the exact time I woke you the first day of the New Year. It was when I said sleep would never be the same. You said I should not seek sleep. That uncertainty would intervene. I didn't ask for an explanation.*
>
> *As night fled into morning, there was an unfamiliar rain. Even in that cleansing, I knew the peace that had passed between us was running through the grates along the street and had already begun to bleed into all lost time.*
>
> *I tell you this because I have no one else to tell.*
> *Lisette.*

I never gave it to him.

Arye had a clear sense of purpose. I needed him to believe in me.

Many years later I met him for a coffee in Lima. He brought news of Rolff and Marta and when he didn't mention Pablo I asked.

He paused.

In that silence I felt the shovel handle clenched between my fingers and my palm all over again. He said, five days after you left, Pablo was found hanging from a fifty-year-old pine tree, a sisal rope around his neck. They strung him up on the outskirts of the village where he was born. His family was afraid to bring the body down. It would have been seen as an act of defiance and there might have been another killing. The dead were warnings written in blood.

And so I saw Pablo as the murderers intended, hanging well beyond the time it took the vultures to tear him to pieces, longer than it took to pick each bone clean, so there would be nothing left of him but the dust from the shit of the animals that had eaten him. That shit would be glued to the Andean soil, dried in the sun that burned during the day and froze each night. That dust of him would be borne in a cool fresh wind. Not until a year or more had passed, then maybe, the family would have gathered the bones and buried him.

What else? I wanted to scream, but sat perfectly calm and asked quietly.

Arye didn't answer.

What?

His eyes were gouged out.

What does that mean?

It could have been his brother that murdered him.

I never heard that before. Is that what *Sendero* required to prove allegiance?

It's complicated. Years later, not far from the hanging, a boy discovered graves of half-charred bones, poorly buried, the bones of children. This was the work of the military, not *Sendero*.

I stared ahead.

Arye said, that is what is presumed when cadavers are found that have been burned and then hastily buried.

Minnie is shaking me; the plants are dying as you daydream, she says.

The ceiling is blue, the walls a sodden ochre.

She leads me from the hallway into the room where the patients are seated under the fluorescent lights. One tube flickers and buzzes until it goes dead. Then the zapping stops.

I like to look inside this room early in the morning. The janitor cleans it each night then swivels shut the Venetian blinds with the grimy cord. Now the room is full of patients, the gray people, and I am one of them. The chair I reach for scrapes the floor the way the teacher's fingernail once scraped the blackboard. These men and women would remember that sound from grammar school. Not the squeaky sound a marker makes across a white board. I want to apologize but stop because I don't think they heard the noise. I am the only one who jumped. Perhaps it is their medicine, but they seem more anesthetized than me.

Bags of soil and many colored plastic planters, Styrofoam cups and flats of ivy line the middle of the table. The man on my left can't keep his hands from shaking. When his cup is half-full, he hits it with the trowel. The dirt spills. I stare at the methodical one; I see him as an assembly line worker, once employee of the year, and think he is afraid to leave his seat. I too am afraid.

Should I select a plant? Or ask someone to pass me a planter? How long did Pablo suffer? Where will I tell Phoebe I got the ivy? Did the military or *Sendero* retaliate against Pablo's brother; was he dead too?

I know I'm not going to get up for the things I need to plant. Planting is for those who can still imagine things getting done.

My chair might make that noise again. The others could be watching.

It would be a good thing to try. The soil running through my fingers might be soft and fine. I can see it is smooth without shards—no bones in there. But I can't move.

We had to slowly sift the spoiled soil off the head of the shovel, tapping lightly on the metal with one foot, gently moving it side to side, filtering it while examining what fell. In all that looking, riveted on the dirt and dust, if we saw something that could be a bone, a piece of tooth or clothing, we would have to run our fingers through the damp, cold earth.

I was afraid I might find a beating heart or an eye that could still see.

In the earth that stuck beneath my fingernails there could be the residue of someone's drool or blood. Urine or shit expelled under fear of death. When we were done for the day, I knew I was taking home a part of someone whom somebody loved.

I shut my eyes and shake my head.

Minnie says my name.

I hold my arms in front of me and make myself look. This is when Minnie puts a cup in front of me.

I jump.

You need to get going. Her voice is firm, we don't have the room all morning.

I look down.

She places a roll of masking tape in the middle of the table. Write your names on the tape. Then put them on the bottom of your planters.

I tear a piece and even though it is crooked and buckled I write in bold black letters: **My name is Lisette.**

Part II

CHAPTER 1

LIMA. Is this you?

Still gray.

I ask Karl if he sees gray or is it that I am still seeing what I remember from when I was here three years ago with Arye, even though I am here again and am no longer working off memory.

It is gray, he says, and the buildings are soot-covered. Even the beautiful colonial ones that encircle the *Plaza de Armas*.

There has been little upkeep, mostly bullets and tanks and soldiers. No one has been planting flowers.

There are more beggar children than I remember, Indians from as far away as the jungle, wearing photographs attached to pieces of cord. Sometimes all they have is a name that dangles: a name, a photograph, this is who is missing. String them together and the names and pictures become stick figures, something like an x on a scorecard. But in saying the name the dead come alive, if only on the lips of the one reciting. A man, a woman, a child: you can tell. An *ito* or *ita* attached to the name says it was a child. *Pablocito. Anita.*

Now there is also a curfew.

I avoid the streets I once walked with Arye. He is still here but now travels without an itinerary. It is his protection.

I explained to Karl why I had to leave, that I could no longer be a witness, an excavator, a grave-digger. This time would be mortar and cement and iron, things that remain. An apple orchard, too. Not just soot and bones in bags.

Karl bought two bicycles first thing. His belonged to an engineer, mine to the engineer's son. They lived in the safe part of Lima but were going home to Nebraska. We did a trial run along perfectly clean streets, past wrought-iron gates and gardens full of flowers. I almost forgot where we were.

In our village, five hours from Lima, we relied on those bikes to get us from place to place. We saw things always a bit higher from the ground, but not as high as if we were traveling by bus. It is from this vantage point I still see the Andes. But now the Andes come to me only in dreams.

If it is a good day I'm on that bicycle again. The mountains are on my left and the jungle is on my right.

Our barn was surrounded by carefully planted rows of wheat, barley and corn. You couldn't see it from the dirt road, only from above.

In the mornings we crooked our necks in order to see the mountains. They were not jagged but a series of the letter U upside down. They were our anchor. Karl spent days climbing. He learned where the streams began and the fastest way to reach the lake. He took a notebook with him. The same one the children used in school, with a map of Perú on front. It was when he allowed himself to make up stories, to collect wild flowers. He wasn't like Arye. He could not live on facts alone.

At first the rain didn't bother us.
Over time water dissolves everything.

•   •   •

Here the asylum roof leaks into a metal pail.

There we took turns dumping pots of leaking roof into fields saturated with standing water. These pools of ink grew larger, bottomless and black with a layer of pesticide residue on top. Sometimes I would see a rainbow there.

It is the custodian's job. He can't rely on us to dump the water. If we don't and it runs over, one of us might fall.

Karl points to a river on the map. When his finger is at the mouth of the Amazon he says, this dot is your head and to the south—see right here—is mine.

I say, the rain is killing me.

It will end. That's why they call it a season.

But the water keeps falling on my papers. The black letters turn gray, then run, settling in and around the letter q.

He buys a typewriter in the market the same day he brings the kitten. The one that dies that night. Before I am awake he has buried it in the valley below the water table, taking into consideration the slope of the land and the source of our drinking water.

This roof must have holes the size of grapefruits. He wants me to laugh.

I can't.

I will sell you for one grapefruit.

Will that get me out of here? At least for the rainy season? I'm pulling my hair into a bun. I use a pencil to hold it in place. My shirt is sticking out from under a layer of sweaters. There are mud and grass stains on my knees.

That wall around you, he hesitates, will weaken and when it does, you will crumble.

* * *

I am feeling hunger. It has been so long I'm not sure this is what it is called. I want potatoes, carrots, garlic and onions and the coarse rice we ate. Even though, by the end, that food sickened me.

The violence moves in like sheets of rain. It comes from the desolate *puna* where wild alpaca graze, where the land is unyielding and the temperature below freezing.

There are men on horses who demand the Indians join. Those who refuse are murdered in the name of Mao. After *Sendero* the military comes. It is the military that tries to hide those it murders.

In the dry season, the Pan American Highway is a path of dust, and in the rainy season a river of mud. Trees and branches from mudslides block the road. The bus stops and the passengers take turns clearing the road, using shovels stored in the baggage compartment. When it is my turn I ask Karl if he will dig for me. I never would have asked Arye.

After the bus is on its way I ask why they don't install metal netting to hold the mountains back, the way they do back home, especially in the places where they had to blast through rock to make the road?

Certain things cannot be held back. Besides they don't worry about what they can't change. Worry belongs to the privileged.

Inside an office without windows I am offered the only other chair. I face the general who is seated across the desk, a wooden surface with nothing on top, no papers or pencils. Enrique, Matias and Karl stand behind me. The general asks, what are you doing with '*them*'?

I look away.

Karl says, last year there was a problem with the seeds. It may have been immunity to the pesticides, or the seeds had expired, but over half of the crop was lost.

There was no problem with the seeds. The general waits.

Karl doesn't say anything.

The general continues, the problem is with the Indians. They have depleted the soil. He tries to dismiss us by averting his eyes. When we do not move, he gets up and opens the door.

We follow *them* to an outdoor market. I choose seats on a wooden bench closest to a wall of ponchos that has been hung to break the wind. Matias and Enrique sit across from us.

I'm sorry, I say.

The air is bitter cold.

Karl offers Enrique his potatoes.

Enrique takes them with his hand.

Matias looks at me. I give him mine.

You don't want them? Enrique asks.

I shake my head no.

I am embarrassed I can refuse food so easily. The truth of my generosity is I saw the cook washing the plates in a barrel of stagnant water. I don't want to be sick on the bus.

We take the back four seats. Enrique and Matias fall asleep as soon as the bus starts moving, each leaning into the other.

Enrique brings us carrots. Karl cleans each one with precision, using the spigot in the yard, rubbing them to loosen the dirt. He places one next to the other on the wooden board so they will dry in the sun.

I offer Enrique a tea. He and Karl follow me into the barn.

What is Washington? Enrique asks.

I point to it on the map and then to New York. This is where I'm from, I say.

The coast?

Yes, and Karlos is from here. I show him the round circle that is Chicago. It doesn't have an ocean—just this, a great lake. His father wanted him to become a basketball player so he could be rich.

I hand Karl the graphs I have been working on.

He says to Enrique, we are just about ready to submit our proposal.

Enrique asks, where is the money for the factory really coming from?

The U.S. government. It had been allocated for Nicaragua. I point to it on the map. But then the U.S. changed its mind. That's why we got it.

Like that? They just took it away? Enrique sits on the bench near our propane stove and places his hat on the wooden table. They could take it from us too?

In English Karl says, your graphs are wrong.

I don't answer Enrique's question. I'm looking directly at Karl.

Enrique looks up. He doesn't understand but sees my reaction and hears the silence.

What I want to say next, but don't, is my father withheld dinner until I was able to recite the day's math. That was after he said I was stupid. I'm remembering when he hit me over the head with my school ruler, the one with the metal edge, until my forehead bled.

The money arrives in Lima. It is at the U.S. embassy.

Karl gives a wad to Enrique.

The village builds the factory.

Things are going to change.

Nothing changes.

We call a meeting to organize the first twenty workers. Only the men volunteer. I look at Enrique. He says, the women aren't going to work in the factory.

What? Someone will come from Washington, from the agency that has given you the money and when they see no women they'll want to know why. They will want the money back.

It's how we do things. Enrique says.

No, I tell him.

We'll take a vote, Karl says.

The women don't raise their hands.

I am angry when I leave the meeting. It is still raining.

Karl comes home an hour later.

I offer him a towel.

He shakes his head no.

Lisette, they trust you. You weren't fair. You just dismissed them.

He closes the bedroom door.

CHAPTER 2

AT SUNSET we gather in Enrique's courtyard. His house is the best in the village although only half-finished. In the two years we live here, the holes where windows should have been are never filled.

The radio is set to the only station. It carries a soap opera from Venezuela. The soap opera, the money from the United States, Karlos and I, who just walked into their village and stayed, and who in time left, one without the other—are only a few of the many things that do not make sense.

Tomorrow we will go to the hot springs, Enrique says. It is where the sick come to be healed, where women give birth without pain.

We drive two hours. It begins to snow. Steam billows from the ground as a streak of light breaks through the clouds.

I have seen the power of the Andean sun, the way it can sheave glacial ice and set it free. With my palm open, I catch one flake. If I could just hold it this way, but as soon as it falls it melts and is gone.

I follow Enrique's wife, Amparo, and the other women. At a distance from the men they begin to undress and so do I. I cling to a shrub alongside the pit and ease my frozen toes into the water. The mud sucks me down. I am thinking Fatima and Lourdes as I sink into the simmering cauldron. If it is brewing hepatitis, typhoid or cholera I have no immunity.

The men are off to the side. Karl's head bobs above the water. His is the only blonde one. I have never seen the men without their hats before.

Amparo looks at me and asks straight out, how come you don't get babies?

I take pills. The pills prevent a baby from forming.

They don't believe me. I don't know how to say intercourse in Quechua. Our missionary tutor, the pastor from North Dakota with the pimples and starched shirt, must have known. We never asked.

We want that medicine, Amparo says, get it for us.

I promise.

Blanca comes to the *cuyera* most nights for English lessons. Karl plays the flute or bakes cookies while we sit in front of picture books. She tells me she will be twelve next week.

At the end of the hour, Enrique comes for her. He hands me a package wrapped in rough brown paper. He is smiling, Amparo made this for you.

Inside is a bag woven in many colors. My name is sewn along the side in red thread. She spells it **Liset**.

Illuminated by the single bulb I see Blanca has Enrique's face, almost exactly.

He asks, who will go to the market to sell the sacks?

You, I say.

He doesn't answer.

Blanca stares at me.

It's an honor.

No. You will go. Enrique looks at Karl.

Karl asks, what will you do when we're not here?

We will build you a house. Better than the one you are in now.

We can't stay forever, I say.

Enrique pauses. No, he says. Just until you die.

But it's the village's project. They are your looms; the sacks you have woven belong to you. If you begin to sell in the market then others from nearby villages will follow. The money you bring in will help pay down the loans on the land.

He shakes his head, Indians don't sell in that part of the market. We are the only Indians to make these sacks because of the money that came from your government.

The color drains from Karl's face.

I take a breath, Enrique, there comes a time when things must change. You can bring about change. We will go with you but you will sell them.

Enrique's eyes go dead.

Blanca will not look at me.

CHAPTER 3

IT WRAPS ITSELF around me. Exhaustion and dread and I am shaking.

We fell asleep earlier than usual last night. It was the cold. I'm not sure who woke first or if we woke at the same time but it was to a chorus of all the dogs in the village barking, followed by a screeching sound, the kind I have heard only pigs make. We stayed in bed on our backs and did not move. Holding each other's hand, we stared at the ceiling, not seeing anything, that's how dark it was, we just listened. Morning came.

The water is set to boil for coffee. I am on my way outside to use the latrine. I open the door but do not move. At the bottom of the hill where the dirt path leads to the Pan American Highway, I see them.

Hanging from the trees.

The dogs, with their entrails scooped out and left on the ground.

Flies are everywhere and vultures too.

Karl, hurry.

He stands alongside me and looks out. The village must know. I'll go see. Stay here.

I pace. Then kick at the soot and dust on the floor. I pull my hair and bite my nails.

It takes Karl twenty-seven minutes to return.

Blood drips from the eucalyptus leaves when the wind blows.

Karl says I exaggerate.

Later he asks, is there blood in my hair?

I can't look, not for blood. Don't make me think there might be dogs' blood glued to your scalp or to the shafts of blonde. What happened last night?

Sendero raided the village. Enrique says the village had been ordered to join them and it refused. This morning they were afraid to take the dogs down. But by the time I got to the school they decided they had no choice. They are afraid of retaliation. The *cabildo* divided the village into sections. Some will cut the ropes and shovel the dogs into piles. Others will dig the graves.

I hear the children crying. Across the way women are huddled behind the unfinished windows of their houses. The front gates to the houses are still closed.

The path to the Pan American is empty. The only people outside are the men working with the dogs.

I haven't left the *cuyera*. When Karl comes home again I see blood on his boots.

Go back down and wash your shoes in the irrigation ditch.

They cracked the pipes, Lisette. The water isn't running and what water there is, isn't clean.

Find some that isn't blood-stained. Wash your shoes before you bloody our path or the house.

He sees I don't understand, knows I won't understand even if he says it again. I watch him walk back down to the ditch. I call after him, are you sure, can we be sure —that it is only the blood of dogs?

．　．　．

Chimbo slept inside with us last night. He always does. But when he cried I took him into our bed, even with his fleas. He is one of the few left.

Karl buried Chimbo's mother.

THE NEXT MORNING we eat our bread and butter. I was afraid to go for milk. Usually I buy it from the woman across the way and boil it for fifteen minutes. I get up from the table to go outside to wash the dishes when Karl tells me to sit.

I'm going to leave this morning, he says. One of us has to. I need to see what is happening in the villages above, and if it is the same as what is happening here I need to gather proof. You don't need to come. I know you had enough the first time, with Arye, I won't ask you to do it, not this trip.

I want to tell him no, that he can't go and leave me alone. I am fighting back tears so I don't say anything.

I'd like to take your camera.

I almost say you won't be able to do it. The calm and methodical gathering of evidence will destroy you. You are more like me than you are like Arye. It takes a certain kind of person to do that work. But I don't speak. I do not blink. All I can do is stare.

I'll leave you mine.

I go to bed each night holding a photograph of him in my hand. I rarely leave the *cuyera*. I read most of the day. But I don't remember much. I'm just turning pages.

We never installed a lock on the front door. Now I'm sorry. I think I am safer if I sleep in my clothes.

On the third night Blanca comes to the *cuyera*. I open the door when she says her name. I see Enrique at the bottom of the path. He calls to me, are you all right?

Yes, I tell him.

She says, my father brought me here to stay with you.

Why? I call to him.

Just until Karlos comes back. I don't want you to be alone and I didn't think you would want to leave the *cuyera*. So here, instead, is Blanca.

She smiles.

I need someone, even a child.

I would like that, I tell her. We listen to his footsteps as he walks back across the gravel path. I am hoping I can sleep. I need sleep.

Blanca lies down beside me on the side that is Karl's.

I usually read before bed, do you ever do that?

I don't think she can read in Spanish, not even a picture book with only a few words. I ask if she wants to continue with her English lessons.

She shakes her head no.

I light the candle then offer her Karl's hat, the one with ear flaps in gray and black. Her braid sticks out. Only men wear this type of hat. I have the same one. She probably thinks I look stranger than usual. Green-eyed white-skinned in a man's hat. These hats are the warmest ones we could find that did not itch.

I start a story. It is the beginning I like most.

"Many years later, as he faced the firing squad, Colonel Aureliano Buendía was to remember that distant afternoon when his father took him to discover ice. At that time Macondo was a village of twenty adobe houses, built on the bank of a river of clear water that ran along a bed of polished stones, which were white and enormous, like prehistoric eggs. The world was so recent that many things lacked names, and in order to indicate them it was necessary to point."

I look over at Blanca to see if she likes the story.

She asks me to keep going even though she looks as if she is nearly asleep.

Late in the afternoon of the ninth day of Karl's absence—I am weeding the tomato garden and sense someone watching me. I look up, not sure what I might see. It is Karl. Forgetting for the moment where he's been, I throw the trowel to the side and run down the path. I may have yelled welcome. It didn't seem an inappropriate greeting but I didn't know then what he had seen.

The dried quinoa along the path scratches my face. When I reach him, my arms extended, I am desperate to draw him to me, but I withdraw. He is walking in a sort of sleep.

I gave my poncho away, he says.

I take his knapsack. His forearms are black and blue. There is blood caked beneath his nails. I try to take his hand. He pulls away.

He goes into the bedroom and sits on the bed. I go into the other room to put the water on to boil. By the time the tea is ready he is asleep on top of the blankets, still dressed. I press my fingers against his wrist and feel a faint pulse.

A day later I wake him to spoon soup between his parched lips. He stares ahead. Tells me the seeing is exhausting. He closes his eyes and sleeps two more days.

On the third day he calls me. I am reading *Poems from the Quechua* on the bench beside the stove.

The one I recite out loud is called "War Song."

> "We shall drink from the traitor's skull,
> we shall wear his teeth as a necklace,
> of his bones we shall make flutes,
> of his skin we shall make a drum;
> later, we'll dance."

He is propped up on the pillows. His hair is matted and he smells of mud and dirty wool.

Lisette, in my knapsack are rolls of exposed film. Will you take them to Lima and mail them to New York?

I tell him, I have film too. I went to the village above us. The military conducted a nighttime raid; after that many people fled. They were afraid *Sendero* would come next. I went to see if there was anything left. At first I stayed inside the *cuyera*. Blanca came to sleep with me on the third night. I have pictures of the burnings and of the words scrawled in warning on the stone walls in red. I couldn't dig; I should have. There were bloodied leaves near the grove of eucalyptus trees on the northernmost hillside. This wasn't supposed to be my job, taking photographs and keeping notes. I did this once. Arye still does, but me no, I never wanted to do that again. It's the military the villagers are afraid of, they are sure that is who is responsible.

Mail your film in a different envelope. No, better to divide it into three packets. That way if some is confiscated the rest might get through. Wrap it in a tourist's poncho.

Karl, I need to tell you I walked to where we had picnicked, near the edge of the pine forest where no one lives. There had been a fire, the charred wood was still there, and when I walked in deeper, past the trees, I saw the freshly dug holes. Someone had kicked leaves over them. The photographs won't look like anything. I couldn't dig them up or even walk close. When you are better I will show you so you can do what needs to be done. For now I'll go to Lima first thing tomorrow and be home by night.

It will take longer than a day.

If the buses are running and Lima is not in a blackout, I can do it.

It's the military that burns the bodies. The *cabildo* of the village above told Enrique they have seen them, mostly at night.

CHAPTER 5

I WALK FASTER toward the *cuyera*. The light is on in the bedroom. I run up the path, calling to Karl. I don't want him to be frightened by the noise outside the window.

He's listening to the radio. He looks like a sick pale child with tear-stained cheeks. When I sit down I realize how tense I've been, how my body aches from being so alert, my head too. I mailed everything. I'll pour wine. Then I'll make omelets. Water first. I felt as if someone was following me, that something was going to happen that would keep me from mailing the film and then from getting back home.

Karl takes my hand.

Thank you, I say.

For what?

This is the first time you've touched me since you got back.

I'm better. After I went to the bathroom this morning I sat outside on the bench. The sun I had forgotten, and the view, I want to get back to doing things. But when I went inside I was so tired I slept all day. Later when I woke up I put the radio on. There was music from Brazil playing. I closed my eyes and moved slowly across the floor. I was dancing. I was thinking it's going to be all right.

You're in the clothes you were wearing when you left three

weeks ago. I'll boil water for a sponge bath. It might make you feel better. I know you aren't prepared to hear this, that I will disappoint you, but I am terrified.

I'm not. Not anymore.

What about what you saw?

I expected it, except I would not have thought, I didn't think, the men could do it, it was as if they were raping their sisters, their mothers.

There was no way to stop them?

No.

Don't tell me more.

Our floor is covered in dust. I stand and take the broom and begin sweeping. I use so much force the strands of straw in the head of the broom begin to snap off. I am perspiring even though it is cold inside.

My allergies are bad, I say; it's the dust. It's so much worse this season. The dustpan, where is it? It should be here with the broom. What am I going to do with this pile? I can't just leave it right here where we walk.

Sweep it into the corner. When I get up I'll take care of it. For now if it's off in the corner it won't bother us. Just let it settle. Come here, please, sit next to me and tell me what was it like in Lima.

The military blocked the roads. They banged the Indians' heads against the buses and kicked them in the shins, but we got through. Don't they know *Sendero* doesn't come by road?

BUSES AND CARS are ambushed. Men in camouflage block the roads. There are raids in the mountains, people are rushing to escape although it isn't clear where. They are not aligned with anyone. They want only to survive.

Sendero strengthens its hold.

The military tries to bury what it has done.

The military or *Sendero*?

Some days we hear it is one, then the other.

Enrique brings an egg, apologizes because he only has one. He too hasn't left the village. We have run out of propane but I don't tell him because I don't want him to give us their eucalyptus branches. There isn't much to eat, no one has been to town, all we have are the potatoes, carrots and onions from the fields.

Karl is stronger.

I take his hand. It is still bruised. Does it hurt?

It feels better, but do you think this finger is broken? See how it doesn't go straight?

How did it happen?

There was a raid. He stops and closes his eyes.

And?

My hand was trampled.

I don't believe him. But I don't need to know. Instead I say, are you able to go for a short walk?

We make our way to the center of the village. There are voices behind us. It is Enrique's son, pressing his wife against the outside wall of their mud house, pushing himself into her. Her skirt is off and the fuchsia tie with silver threads lies on the ground at her feet.

They must be drunk.

Seems to me she's enjoying it.

How do you say intercourse in Quechua?

He shakes his head. I don't think we ever knew. Then he points to the mountain in front of us.

You can't, I say. And aren't you too weak?

Come with me.

No. If I leave I will go far from here.

We shouldn't be making decisions now, not from fear.

You said you were no longer afraid.

Lisette, I'm afraid for you. You don't trust yourself or anyone, really. You hide in the familiar but there is no familiar.

A branch snaps.

I think it's a gun.

A child cries.

I imagine the worst, that it is some child's mother being taken away.

When it is dark, especially when there are no stars or moon and the candle has burned, I try to wake him from what looks like more than sleep. I check his breathing. If they were going to come back they would have already come. In the dark it is easier to believe what is not true—this is the case for the good and for the bad.

. . .

I don't stop Karl.

I stand on the hillside and wave. The lupine is in bloom and it is warm like the Northeast in fall. The mountains are framed by a blue sky. Beyond what I can see are all the nearly frozen streams with perfectly clear water.

CHAPTER 7

I ASK FOR ONE PORTION.

The meat woman asks why only one.

Karlos is away.

She invites me to stay with her in the apartment above the store, just until he gets back. She calls me by the name he sometimes uses, *Manchita,* the one who is stained. But he says it lovingly when he comes to me in bed. He wouldn't have said it in front of her. It must be what comes to mind when she sees my face. She doesn't catch herself as I would expect if she were aware of having said something wrong.

This stain, the color of port wine and blood, covers the right side of my face, runs across my eyelid, under my eye, drips onto my lip and oozes along my chin.

I hate the color red.

When I was born my mother left me in the hospital. Eventually my grandmother came for me.

I tell the woman my name is **Lisette**.

The ground meat I buy is wrapped in brown paper. It runs red and stains the paper redder.

She ties it with a piece of string. The kind that looks like peppermint, red and white twisted twine.

I buy fruit and wine at the next two stalls. Not red but white. When Karl is away I drink to get to sleep.

The bus driver slows down at the place in the road where there is silt and fallen branches. When he jams on the brakes we are thrown forward. Potatoes roll down the aisle. I feel something sticky collecting between my legs. It could be the eggs have broken. I do not look. What good would it do? I'm wondering if I should have taken the meat market woman's offer of a room.

Dust from the bus skidding across mounds of soot blows inside. It gets in my eyes and the grit of it wedges between my teeth. As it settles I imagine men in the distance emerging from the grove of trees. This time, though, it is different—they are coming for me. They will use me, the marked one, as a warning. My body will hang from the tree above our *cuyera*. Karl will be on his descent and see a strip of my poncho waving in the breeze. He will wonder why I only washed one piece of clothing. As he continues toward home, the outline of my poncho will become clearer. He will be thinking how exhausting his climb was. But when he gets closer he will see me.

I put the groceries away.

I look at my watch.

I try to read.

I make coffee.

I walk in circles around the tiny room. I see my reflection in the pane of glass and stop to run my fingers across my birthmark. It is raised in one spot. It is bumpy and irregular.

Cain had a mark across his forehead that he could not see or erase, but others saw it. It was a warning.

Hester was marked with a scarlet letter.

Hawthorne wrote, "The Birthmark." I can't remember it exactly. When we forget our stories it is the beginning of losing ourselves. A scientist marries a woman with a birthmark on her face. He thinks she is beautiful at first until he becomes obsessed with the mark. He makes it his life's work to rid her of it. The final elixir makes her sick. The mark fades as she is dying and right before she dies he sees her face smooth and clear.

I decide to do laundry. This way it will be my poncho hanging above the *cuyera*. By midday I am increasingly uneasy. I walk to the schoolyard. The children are waiting in the one room dressed for class.

Is your teacher here? I ask.

No. Just like yesterday and the day before.

One little boy is lying on the floor at the door. I pick him up and sit him in a chair. A dog is milling about inside. Another dog sleeps in a patch of sun.

Do you know the story of Little Red Riding Hood?

They shake their heads no.

Capericita Roja is walking through the forest to her grand-mother's, just like her mother asked. It is a lovely day. The birds are chirping and she hums as she skips, stopping to pick flowers. She prefers the ones called *ñachag* or sometimes *amor seco*. These are the ones with five yellow petals. She has never been able to find one with more or with less. She runs the rest of the way to her grandmother's. She goes inside on tiptoe because it is very quiet. At first she doesn't say a thing. But when *Capericita Roja* sees her grandmother propped up in bed on a pillow she backs away; something has frightened her. When grandmother says, in a voice *Capericita Roja* doesn't recognize, *Capericita Roja, venga aquí,* this gives her a shiver that sets the hair on her arms to rise.

She approaches the bed and as she gets closer . . .

I stop. There is no wolf in that bed and *Capericita Roja* is not

eaten. When they hear the story again I hope they will understand why I lied.

I stay until the teacher would have left. Then walk with
them to the fields. Their mothers and grandmothers are bent
over weeding. We work together and when it is dusk I help
them strap the grass across their backs. The women are stooped
over from the weight. Slowly they make their way up the hill.
I don't know how they can do one more task, this lugging,
and then still prepare dinner. I am exhausted from bending
over the mud, pulling weed after weed, and when I reach the
cuyera, I collapse onto my bed and stare at the mountain outside my bedroom window.

It is the mountain he is on.

CHAPTER 8

I HAVE THIS DREAM.

Coffee cups rattle on the table, shaken by the force of military jets flying back and forth across the same path of sky. Coffee runs down the sides of the cups.

Dark puddles pool on the glass table.

A light seeps out from under the bathroom door. I am in my father's house. School is about to begin. I know I have to get dressed or my father will be angry with me. But the coffee keeps spilling and liquid is running along the floor. I want to finish dressing but first I have to wipe every drop.

My father will hurt me if the coffee keeps doing this, if the kitchen is a mess and breakfast isn't served. I am up to my ankles in coffee. I call for mother. There is no mother.

When I look down I am standing in a river of blood.

CHAPTER 9

THE FIRST Catholic church in this country is at the entrance to the next town over. Its ceiling is made of reeds from the river. A mural on the inside wall tells the story of the conquest. Inside it I am safe even though the door is open to the wind. Behind a pane of glass are dried flowers from long ago and many small caskets stacked on top of each other. An evangelical minister and his community are building a new church here, three times the size of the old one, with stained glass windows and a steeple that reaches into the sky.

Karl and I had spoken with Enrique about reconfiguring the flow of the river for irrigating the land so the Indians in our village might not be so poor. I want the minister to help. He might, for in the helping he will see an opportunity to gather more souls.

He is from one of the Dakotas, the one with the faces of men carved into the mountains. He has come with the hope of scratching his face into the Andes just that way.

I am drinking coffee the minister's wife has prepared, hoping maybe they can protect me. I do not think this because they are white, or because they present themselves as being connected to God. It is that I am afraid.

Last night the pigs squealed and I was terrified it was the noise of the few dogs that survived.

In the kitchen I am gripped with a new fear. It might be dangerous for me to be here. The evangelicals have mobilized the Indians against *Sendero*. If I'm not already marked, this visit could be decisive. I'm sweating now, wishing I'd gone with Karl. I hear him telling me not to worry, that after all the worry, what it comes down to is this thing called fate.

This preacher whose name I don't know has a wife who looks like him. She keeps pouring coffee and I keep drinking. This is what it is like back home, always enough, always too much. Would he have left her for two nights, especially when in those two nights so much was hanging in the balance?

Their house seems like a house back home. I excuse myself to use the bathroom. In addition to the toilet, bath and sink, it has its own heater. I turn the faucets on and off. They do not leak or gush or drizzle but provide a steady and directed stream. I can not resist sitting on the toilet seat, not because I have to go, not even after all the coffee, just to sit.

When I get up I rummage through their cabinets and steal a box of Tampax—even though I don't use Tampax and do not want to need Tampax. I am afraid to bleed. Their god must see this stealing going on—their god is not *Sendero's* god or the god of my village—so this act will go unpunished. No harm will come from this theft of a thing I don't even like to use, that I don't think I will ever use, not even here where I am accustomed to making do.

When I was younger and wanted to be older I imitated my grandmother by taking the paper inserts from the Tampax and taping them together to make one long cigarette. I practiced being an adult and in my grandmother's gold Plymouth, which had a plastic sunflower wrapped around the antennae and windows that rolled up and down, I allowed myself to imagine

I was in control. That I was able to drive away. I'm sure the preacher man and his wife have a pickup truck with power windows and even a radio, too.

Time to get out of the bathroom. I'm sure by now my coffee is cold, too cold to finish but I don't believe in waste, not in these parts.

I am thinking Karl should be making his way down the mountain now. I don't want to go home until he's there or Blanca is going to have to sleep with me again. I don't know how to say in Quechua, you must stay or I will fall apart so instead I will say, please don't go.

I've seen madness in the Andes. You can't help but see things here you don't see at home because here they don't hide them away, the cleft palates, the club foots, the insane.

There is a boy in this village. He stands in the road and calls out insults in Quechua. He isn't violent, just loud. His mother says he talks too much. This is why he cannot go to school. There must be a word for mad but she doesn't use it. I wonder if she thinks it, maybe, just once in a while.

I leave the bathroom. It's already been too much time. They might think I have dysentery and be sorry they invited me in. Not that dysentery per se is contagious. Cholera for example, which can give you the runs, is. But the dysentery I once had was from parasites, and this I wouldn't be able to give to them unless my hands had somehow become contaminated and then I touched the food they later ate. Right now I don't have dysentery. What I have is fear and although this is contagious I do not think they are worried. Perhaps they really believe God is looking over them, that somehow they are exempt. The villagers have come to accept that the preacher and his wife have moved in with their possessions, the likes of which have no translatable names in Quechua.

They have built a radio tower on the highest hill, broadcasting prayers over a local radio station, day and night. Enrique says the villagers don't pay much attention to the preaching and there are songs he likes.

There is a song I know but this one is in real Quechua, not evangelical Quechua. It was sung many years ago, way before they knew what an evangelical was going to look like. If Karl were here I would recite it for him. It is called "Song":

Prince

Because you're a star
    yes
you shine at night
    yes
under the sun's fire
    yes
I'll never see you
    yes

Princess

If I'm a star
    no
open your heart
    no
and under the sun's fire
    no
half-close your eyes
    no

Prince

You seem to call
    yes

only in moonlight
    yes
and when I come near
    yes
you change into snow
    yes

Princess

If I seem to call
    no
please come quickly
    no
if I change into snow
    no
toss me your fire
    no

Prince

When my fire burns you
    yes
you change into dew
    yes
are you the wind
    yes
or are you a dream
    yes

Princess

If you think I am dew
    no
bring your lips near
    no

> though I may be a dream
>   no
> don't ever lose me
>   no

The minister tells me he has a water plan.

More coffee please, but no thank you to the plan that will not work, stealing water from the lake without replenishing it.

I don't ask if caffeine is forbidden. I think that is a Mormon thing. I don't want to know because I don't want their glossy brochure. There has to be a lot of caffeine in this coffee. Caffeine or something that feels like it is running in my blood.

CHAPTER 10

HE ISN'T BACK.

It has been more than two days and two nights. And that was all he said it would be, two days and two nights.

In the afternoon I do laundry with the women. They laugh at me and it is true I don't know how to do the wash without washing myself. After changing my shirt for the second time, I put on Karl's rain poncho. It's inefficient and wasteful but I have trouble keeping the water from sloshing over me, wave-like. A head-to-toe sort of drowning.

Without warning three men arrive. Enrique wants me to go with him because he thinks they are lying.

Who are they, if not who they say?

They are military.

As I am collecting my hat and putting on my boots I ask, why aren't they in uniform? Could they instead be from the bank in Lima, the men who still own your land, the ones that hold the mortgages?

That's not who these men are. And if they really were from the bank, why now?

It could be to see how much damage was done when the ir-rigation pipes were cracked.

Whenever they come from Lima it costs us money. But these men aren't from the bank.

You don't recognize them?

No.

Nearly everyone in the village has gathered. We follow the men across the fields. They scour each segment. They want to know who is the head of the *cabildo*. If they were from the bank they would not have to ask. I'm quite sure they are not answering in order to intimidate us. I try again. The other one says, we are getting our bearings.

That night before bed I latch the door.

The nightmares come, vivid scenes of burning bones and blood-soaked wool.

CHAPTER 11

MY NIGHTMARES could be from fever. How high my temperature is I'm not sure. I can't get up for the thermometer. I'm shivering with cold and my throat is burning.

Did the men bring disease? Is anyone else feeling this way? Is this the beginning of an epidemic and when will Karl be home? He would know where I left the thermometer.

CHAPTER 12

I AM FALLING, but, cannot land.

I'm not desperate for aspirin but I am dreaming of water, of many glasses of cold water with perfectly formed ice cubes. I reach for one and begin drinking. Bringing the sweating glass to my forehead, I lean into it, allowing it to cool my burning skin.

I need more and more water. I extend my hand because someone is offering another glass. But the hand darts away. I wait for it to return. Then there is no one handing me anything.

There is a glass off to the side. Even though I can't be sure the water is clean, that it has been boiled for fifteen minutes, I start drinking, then guzzling, so fast the liquid runs down my chin and pools in a semi-circle on top of my collar-bone. I am colder than I ever was, even at the top of the mountain that time we were caught in the snowstorm, when I thought we might not make our way back.

As I near the bottom of the glass I see a snake coiled. It shoots its tongue forward. It is my screaming that wakes me, but not enough. The body, I once read, has a way of protecting itself from pain by shutting down in one way or another when there is no other way to escape. I am still asleep now running past cement block houses because I am not safe. On the wall are names scrawled in red. I see my name and Blanca's. It is the same red the guerrillas use. This is their color because it mimics the color of blood. Or maybe it is blood. Blood is cheaper than red paint.

Through the partially opened door I see a man's foot. I want to know why the military man is not wearing combat boots. But they don't always have supplies. There is a rifle, resting at his side. In his hand is a pencil and he is writing on pages clipped to a wooden board. The date is January 1, 1983, and his entry says,

> Indian women who do not turn over their children are
> whores.

He is on his feet walking toward me. There is no Blanca. He catches me by my hair, a whole clump of it, enough for my mother to gather in a ribbon and tie in a bow, but there is no mother and my grandmother never would have bothered. He pulls me backwards and orders me to stand alongside the chair. My fingers tighten around the frame as he bends me at the waist, my stomach pressed against this very hard thing.

I pretend I am a table.

Tables do not feel pain.

If you must I will allow you to eat off my back. But I have no control to authorize any one thing.

Place your cold metal utensils and tin bowl on the curve of me. I will try not to jerk. Rather, I will let my ribs rise and fall gradually even though I know you are reaching for your knife. I will breathe steadily as you follow the outline of the tangled rope that runs up my spine. Cut gently, I do not want to feel pain. I can see, if I crane my neck to the left, that it is a hunting knife with a carved handle, no, nothing at all like a butter knife.

What color is the blanket? He twists my head and makes me

look. See how red—I will not stop, not until your skin, your body, burn that color. That way you will know you are alive. That way you will feel how much it hurts to be alive.

I'm having trouble catching my breath.

Water, I beg, please.

He turns away from me. For this moment I hope I can escape. I need him to lose his focus. He is facing the door I came through.

I'll give you water he says as he turns back to look at me, then pulls me by my wrist and drags me to the shower.

I am very cold. I think it is the end because he is allowing me to shower. The water's too hot, then freezing. I cannot get clean. I can escape if I get him to do something else. So I talk: the Argentine government took prisoners of the state to the showers after weeks of not bathing. They were allowed to lather under warm water and when covered in soap the guards ordered them out and made them dress in their filthy clothing. The harsh detergent burned through their skin. Imagine, a woman with soap inside her vagina burning through the soft tissue, the agony of it and no remedy, no recourse.

When he goes for the bar of soap to shove up my vagina I will run for the door. This is not what he does. He pulls me from the shower and out of the bathroom, demands I bend over the chair. He is pushing himself inside me from behind, the way dogs do it. He orders me to count to one hundred.

One.

Grandmother had a red wicker basket with a metal closure and inside she kept a pincushion shaped like an apple. There was a green leaf made of felt sewn on top. Alongside the apple that was stuck with pins she lined her spools of thread.

Thirteen.

Perfectly ordered to some sort of logic, the strings wound tightly so they wouldn't tangle. Some were taller than others and wider. In a separate compartment to the left she kept the buttons.

Twenty-four. You couldn't jiggle the box when you brought it down from the cabinet or the buttons might mix with the thread and that would make her angry.

Thirty-one. This is a man's coat button and it is black.

Forty. I see a pearl button from a woman's sweater, and then a metal one I don't know what for or where it came from.

Forty-one. Ugly see-through green plastic . . . that hurts. It was a replacement button for my grandfather's winter coat that was the color of a forest.

I try to block out the sound of his groaning.

Fifty. It is a clear plastic and I like to look through it to see the world outside my grandmother's sewing room.

Whore bitch.

Sixty. I like this one so much. It is a pink rectangle. I would always ask whose it was and if she couldn't remember, which she never could, I would ask if we could make it mine because if it were mine I would not lose it. I see it belonging to a pink sweater with a lace collar and there will also be, somewhere, a matching skirt. That skirt will have a scalloped hem. And this outfit would have been mine, not something my sister once wore. It would have been a birthday present that came in the mail. Once the outside wrapping was torn and lying on the ground I would move on to the box inside. It would be tied with a large and floppy bow with polka dots.

Seventy. No Grandma, it's the pink one I like. Where is it from? Grandmother never remembers anything important, only what she thinks is important.

What he says is, you can't go. Not until it is done.

Until all the men, the fathers, the sons and the husbands see that you are an Indian-loving whore. Your face, he says, has the handprint of the devil, all that red on only one side. Do you know what that means? He hits me on the red side of my face and the thrust of his weight and that slap are so hard I hit the wall.

He says ninety-nine. This button I am showing you is brown like everything else that dies in the fall.

CHAPTER 13

I'LL BE BETTER tomorrow and by tomorrow Karl will be back. What day is it? Is it day already?

Blanca wants to know how to make tea.

I hear her looking for the matches to light the propane stove. When she brings the tea to me with some bread I can't eat. It hurts to swallow even the clear liquid.

Where are your dry clothes?

I point to the red box.

Hold my neck. She pulls me up and helps me into something dry and clean.

I say in English, be my daughter.

CHAPTER 14

KARL ASKS if I know what day it is.

I've been sick since you left.

Thanksgiving.

How do you know?

A mountain climber from Wyoming.

Can't be true, no one lives in Wyoming.

There were snowstorms both days.

We finish our chicken and quinoa.

He takes the flashlight and his knapsack, let's go to the hammock to finish the wine.

It's too late.

It's a beautiful night, perfectly clear. We'll only go as far as the stone marker. I'll bring a blanket for us to sit on.

No. It's not safe.

It's our backyard.

It's too far.

Lisette, they don't need night. If they are going to come, it can be at any time and it won't matter if we are inside or out.

I follow him into the night. We go all the way to the hammock. It hangs between two pine trees; it is my favorite spot. Karl lies on the side that is red. I am on the green. He bought the hammock in the jungle the week I stayed in Lima. The jungle did not interest me, not like the mountains. I prefer the cold and I need to see the sky. He passes me the wineskin he bought in Spain. I was in Spain that year too, but we didn't know each other then.

There are other places I want to see.

He says, Machu Picchu. Lake Titicaca.

Karl, I wonder if the reeds along Lake Titicaca are like the reeds in the next village. But it's Machu Picchu I want to see.

The trains in this country are crammed with pigs and vendors of *choclo*.

Atacama, I say. I want to go where they have found mummies preserved by the sun, the dust and the dry heat, even though the bodies were not wrapped, the way they were in Egypt.

CHAPTER 15

KARL AND I see them as they wind down the mountain behind our house. They go to Enrique's, knowing who he is and where he lives. We think they have listened to Enrique when they do not stay.

Men gather in front of Enrique's house. The women have gone to the fields with their wool and young children. Most are not working but are talking.

When dusk comes I have the feeling the sun may not rise tomorrow. This is before I learn Enrique is missing.

Sendero is encamped in the *puna*. It is estimated they are somewhere between twenty to thirty miles north. The military is not far. The military does surveillance and it is not always precise. They don't think they need to be, for them *Sendero* is everywhere.

Matias says we will meet in the church the next morning, after the cows have been milked.

Karl and I don't sleep. We lie in bed with the candle flickering. Each time it burns down one of us lights another. This is how I know both of us are never asleep at the same time.

In the morning there is no meeting. The guerrillas got here first and rounded up and tethered the sheep outside Enrique's. I hear the children and Blanca screaming. This is when Karl and I start to run toward Enrique's house. At the entrance we are face to face with a man carrying a rifle. He uses it to block the door then points it into the crowd. It isn't until a few minutes later, after I've caught my breath and after they have let Karl inside, that I see all the men have guns.

Amparo, I call. Amparo, are you in the house?

Enrique's brother pushes the guard to the side. Another man, one who had been standing behind the rabbit cage, shoots Enrique's brother between the eyes.

I hear Karl speaking inside. Don't hurt them, they are only children. We will give you what you want, but not the children.

The soldier laughs, I bet this white man here has fucked the Indians, why else would he care so much? Has Enrique given you permission?

Karl says, the rabbits are out back. The *cuyes*, too.

If he can fuck the Indian women, why can't we?

There is plenty of food. You can eat and then you will go.

When he comes outside he is holding the children's hands.

Where's Amparo?

Karl doesn't answer.

The men with guns are speaking quickly then they go door to door. When they are done with one house, they torch the thatch roof and move to the next. Flames engulf the laundry hanging on ropes strung between the trees. Most of the Indians stand back and watch, but others rush about with their children and possessions, trying to grab one last thing. Then everyone is pushing to get away from the thickening smoke.

I do not remember why, if I heard something or someone told me, but I am running to find the little girl next door. I pass the oldest woman in the village hiding behind a stack of wood. Her face is streaked with ash. She is pointing toward the rabbit cage. I find her granddaughter huddled inside. The child's hair is singed and fiery burns cover her right cheek. She is too stunned to cry.

By night the fires have died down. We use water from the irrigation ditches to put out the last of the smoldering embers. The water is contaminated with pesticides and herbicides; the flames turn a deep violet.

The village huddles in the church for the night. It is decided Karl and I will leave at dawn. We will stop at the regional police headquarters. Depending on what they tell us we will continue looking for Enrique or anyone who can help us find him.

That night I tell Karl everything I learned from Arye. I don't think Karl has the strength of Arye, the capacity to respond swiftly and without emotion. I don't tell him he will have to skip over the emotion part or else he will make mistakes.

We go back to the house and I search through my desk. I find my identification papers from before, plus pages of notes with names of contacts. Then, these documents were enough, now I am no longer sure.

The police station has been firebombed. Beneath the charred walls in red paint it says, down with the repression! Defend the lives of the prisoners of war!

Although we will get into Lima past curfew, we do not want to delay our departure until morning. We decide if the buses are running we will go.

The bus slows then stops. There is a roadblock of men with guns. Five soldiers board the bus, and when the Indian man seated beside me does not wake up, the soldier jabs the butt of his gun into the man's chest and forces him off the bus. In the ravine they make him strip naked. One soldier kicks him to the ground. Another soldier comes out from the bushes carrying a huge rock which he uses to crush the Indian's skull.

The tallest soldier is asking Karl for our papers.

The soldier turns the pages. When he is done, he walks slowly toward the back of the bus studying each face. When he stares at me, I feel guilty of whatever he accuses.

The last soldier on the bus searches through the metal box where the driver keeps the slips of all the fares. He orders the man in charge to give him the money. Then he says get going. The bus driver closes the door and starts the engine.

Karl gets up from his seat. What about the man, his things?

Don't bring him on the bus, the driver says. If you do they will come after me. Hurry but just leave his sack alongside of him.

Karl goes outside and bends over the body. I can't see what he is doing.

The bus driver honks.

Karl gets back on.

Is he alive?

Karl doesn't answer.

Is he alive?

Karl puts his head in his hands.

The bus driver puts in a tape. Then turns up the volume. Much too loud. It is a love song playing in Mexican-sounding Spanish.

Part III

CHAPTER 1

LIMA. What has happened to you?

There are no lights as far as we can see. Passengers from other buses are asleep on the steps. We hear reports of looting in the city center. There is no choice but to spend the night with them outside the terminal.

We share two secrets:

One man is dead.

Not one of us did anything.

The sun rises. There are no street vendors, no women in the outdoor market. Shop windows are broken and cars have been firebombed.

A taxi takes us to the center of the city. The driver says, there has been no electricity for three days. He points to the destruction. Most is recent, within the past twenty-four hours. Water is intermittent. Many restaurants and businesses are closed. He drops us at a hotel near the *Plaza de Armas* that he knows is still open.

Karl is tired and wants to rest. I am too nervous to sleep. Every sound makes me jump. He sleeps upright in a chair while I keep watch. When the sun goes down, curfew begins.

There are no people.

Then from the darkness, waking Karl, we hear the echoing, the throbbing sound the women make with their pots and pans as they strike them against the pavement. Into the long night.

The conquerors left the copper, taking the best of the silver and all of the gold. The gold and silver is in museums in Europe and government buildings in Spain and in homes with too many rooms to count. Some has been reconfigured to rococo and filigree. It doesn't say where it came from, that it was mined by the Indians who once owned the land, who chewed coca leaves to stave off cold and hunger, not knowing when the mine might collapse.

This sound of metal to stone cannot be mistaken for anything else. These women are the wives, the daughters and sisters, the mothers of the disappeared. It is in the eerie darkness of dusk, that time between living and dying, when their banging begins, summoning those who cannot come. The pots are not needed to prepare the evening meal. The missing go hungry. Those who wait do too.

The refrain is the same, the howling of many children, and as the night goes on their cries grow louder against ringing copper, in this, a Latin American fugue.

CHAPTER 2

EL CUARTEL GENERAL DEL EJÉRCITO is a modern building that looks as if it is built on sticks, surrounded by gray haze. There are no windows. I ask Karl if the Pentagon has windows. We are standing on the pitted gravel in front of *El Cuartel*, facing each other. This place could be the moon for all the craters and stones and dust. Dust falls and settles on our shoulders. The street is perfectly still but for the moving silt.

We need to go inside, Karl says.

What good will that do?

We need something from them, a formal request, access.

Access?

To the prisons. Karl pulls a piece of paper from his pocket. At least to these, the ones listed. Even if we can't find Enrique maybe we can find someone from the raid.

We work our way through from one office to the next, each with a steel desk nailed to the floor. The authorization has seals and stamps and blue letters in script. Each stamp costs more and when they ask we pay in dollars. A guard takes us to an underground prison. There is nearly no light. I look beyond the rusted bars and filthy windows to faces so swollen it is difficult, nearly impossible, to see where the eyes might have been. But no eyes are better than eyes. It is the eyes that follow me.

There are black and blue faces caked in blood. Some are fresh and oozing, wounds from stabbings and beatings, gunshots, too. I smell rotting flesh, which is different from burning skin or hair. I now know the difference.

We are not allowed to enter the room off the main corridor. From under its door comes the smell of excrement, and it is where the screams begin. I ask the guard in a whisper to tell me, please, what it is that is happening in there.

There is a metal bed and water. We strap them down and apply electricity to different parts of their bodies. They tell us what we need to know. A war is on. It is the only way you might find your friend. The cries grow louder. I can't tell if they are from men or women.

We keep going, moving through the passageways. In the next row are prisoners so young they could be nine or ten years old. It is forbidden to say anything to them. I think maybe they can no longer talk. It could be they have forgotten the words, or there are no words, or could it be that their tongues have been cut out?

Karl, wouldn't you bleed to death?

What? he asks.

If they cut out your tongue wouldn't you bleed to death?

CHAPTER 3

WAVES POUND against the rocky shoreline. A Peruvian Alcatraz.

Each time I hear them crash ashore, I jump.

Even when we are deep inside the prison and under, I hear the waves breaking through.

I cannot keep up. Karl asks the soldier if he can bring me outside. It is agreed I can have a break and then after a few minutes of fresh air we will go back and finish.

The sunlight brings on a blindness I have known only with migraines. I look to where Karl's voice is coming from and I interrupt him, I can't keep this up. Today I am still able to look into the eyes of the prisoners. I see nothing or else I see terror. There isn't anything in between.

When it is over and we are standing outside, finished for the day, Karl and I say, we will never find Enrique.

CHAPTER 4

ONE MORE.

Karl insists. It takes a few days to travel to Puno. If he weren't pushing me, I would have given up already.

At nearly thirteen thousand feet my teeth chatter.

A guard leads us through. We could be walking the same corridor the whole five hours, around and around. And in all the faces we do not find Enrique.

WE HAVE NO NEWS, Karl tells Amparo. But we will keep looking. It's possible he's nearby, that he hasn't been taken to prison. He could be with *Sendero*. Maybe he is playing along and one day he will walk away and come home.

You didn't find anyone who saw him? Amparo asks.

No. But they wouldn't let us speak to the prisoners, not unless we saw someone we knew or someone we could identify. Karl touches her shoulder and says, something will change. It can't go on this way forever.

Amparo motions for us to follow her behind the stone wall. Flies are everywhere. There is a strand of plastic beads hanging from a nail. She says to Karl, I need a body so I can bury him.

We don't know if he is dead. We aren't done looking. It's too early to give up.

He's not being sincere. I hear it in his voice and so does Amparo.

She hands Karl the poncho Enrique wore when he worked in the fields.

Karl shakes his head. No, he will come home and need it.

You must take it, and there is something else. Matias was gone for four days. When he came back his hair was gone. He said men tied him to a chair and put a light bulb over his head.

They never turned the light off and it burned through to his scalp. It must have been nearly touching his skin, otherwise how could it have burned that way? Light doesn't do that to hair.

Who took him?

No one knows but when he came back his left arm wasn't working.

What do you mean?

It doesn't move straight. She swings her arm back and forth. It just hangs there like it might fall off. We asked what had happened. All he said was they tied his hands together with a cord and then hung him that way from the ceiling. His feet didn't reach the floor.

Where is he now?

He stays inside most of the time. But his wife says he told her that the men made him give them names and he was afraid for Cholo and Lobo, he said he might have named them.

Cholo and Lobo.

But he wasn't sure. He said he couldn't be sure because he couldn't remember. He said these things when he wasn't feeling right.

I don't believe he gave them names.

It has to be true or at least he thinks it's true because when he came back the first thing he did was go to Cholo's. He told Cholo to leave the village, that there wasn't time to take anything. He was crazy the way he was talking. It wasn't just that Cholo had to leave, he said the whole family had to go. That if any one of them stayed, they would be at risk. He said the same to Lobo.

Cholo and Lobo aren't *Senderistas*.

They are gone now. No one will move into their houses even though they are the better ones. The next day the army came. They took Mono and his brothers. All five are gone.

When?

A few days ago.

Now people are moving closer to the center of the village, near the school, setting up makeshift houses thinking it is safer if we are all together. *Sendero* brings the military. The military brings *Sendero* and we never know when.

I pour wine and drink a glass. It is red from Chile. The color of the blood that keeps spilling. I ask Karl what we are going to do.

He pours himself wine. Do?

I can't stay.

We can't leave.

Is there more wine?

Lisette, we can't leave them.

At least we should move into town. We can come every day.

You think like a child. Do you believe that if you close your eyes, because you can't see them, they can't see you? It doesn't work that way. I'm not leaving, not on the off chance that living in town will protect us. We have no way of knowing. It might put us in even greater danger.

How?

It might be an admission.

Of what?

They think we can protect them.

That isn't true.

We don't know that. Our presence could be a deterrent.

Or a magnet. Maybe we've endangered them by living here.

This can't go on.

They will kill us. And they will kill them. You don't think they're coming back?

If they are there's nothing to do now to change that.

You're wrong. Today we're here. Tomorrow might be too late. You aren't making sense.

Lisette, this is why you shouldn't be making decisions now.

When then? When I close my eyes I see the prisoners. Especially the faces of the children. Don't tell me you don't see them too. I wonder where Enrique is, how they killed him. I don't know how we can keep this up after what we've seen, after not having done anything. I'm afraid of what is stuck in my mind.

Karl gets up abruptly, Lisette, come with me. I have to find a way to forget the smell of burning flesh. We'll go for a few days to the lake. I have never insisted before. I can't leave you here and it is all I can think of to do.

There is the next morning.

I am ready for the possibility there might not be a next. Before the sun is up, I walk with Karl to the base of the mountain. The fields are covered in fine dew. Spider-webs catch the first glimmers of morning light as the sun rises to a perfectly clear Andean sky. After an hour, as the slope becomes steeper, I stop.

Karl, I'm not going on, I'm too tired.

When he no longer sees me, I turn and run to our house, pack one bag, my camera and the negatives. I scribble a note but can't remember what it said or if I tore it up before I hitch-hiked to the nearest town.

I catch the first bus to Lima.

The next afternoon, around the time I estimate he's reaching the summit, I see the outline of skyscrapers through a dense covering of clouds, the way they rise up from the tip of Manhattan, anchored in landfill, surrounded by waterways connecting continents to continents.

Part IV

CHAPTER 1

AN ENVELOPE arrives addressed to me. Inside are photographs Karl took of ice and snow. Now I know I left the note I wrote that morning.

The bicycle I buy on Third Avenue is midnight blue. The same color as the one I left leaning against the *cuyera* wall.

When the sky turns black, the way it does in a summer squall, I am standing at the fence that encircles the reservoir in Central Park. I do not look for shelter. Instead I slide my fingers between the gaps in the wire mesh. Their fingers were smaller than mine, attached to broken bones covered by torn flesh.

Rain falls into my eyes. The east and west sides of Manhattan look as if they are the same distance from where I am standing. I will always be looking for that equidistant point, that nearly mid-mark on the equator.

I try to collect one drop of warm rain. What I want is to preserve it the way it falls. Perfectly round. It hits my palm and runs uninterrupted for the length of the gullies alongside the raised veins in my wrist. I watch it bleed into my sleeve.

I am not going back.

.   .   .

Claps of thunder make me jump. When they die down and the lightning comes, I look at the rest of us standing at the reservoir. No one else has been to the Perú I have seen. For them it is a New York storm in summer, the kind that passes quickly without leaving more than broken branches and fallen leaves.

Crater-like circles of rain form in the black gravelly soot. The bicycle skids and I fall. I should get up but instead roll over to look at the dark sky. The wetness seeps through my clothing, I feel it against my back. The trees are thick with summer, their trunks wide with age. Torn candy wrappers are crumpled in the grass and to my left I see an empty water bottle and a page from the *New York Times*. It is the Sunday crossword puzzle nearly finished. I pull a twig to release the page and inch toward it. I am checking to see if the person who filled in the blanks knew the answers. There are so many words, so many ideas, so much I don't know.

Only a few of us are outside in the rain. There are places nearby to take cover and most everyone has. I try to get up and when I am on my knees I hold the position. There is a certain kind of animal trap that shackles an animal, requiring it to eat off the limb that is caught in order to set itself free. I don't know what comes first, hunger, or the desire to run.

Karl and I had knelt alongside our flowering potato plants with our ears pressed against the soil.

He said, I know you hear the sound of the plants growing.

No. I hear voices.

He took my hand and said things I wanted to hear, things I won't hear again. He led me inside our barn. His woolen poncho smelled like wet sheep.

CHAPTER 2

I HAVE NO USE for this lovely felt hat the women in my village gave me. Blanca selected the embroidered ribbons in orange, purple and blue because they matched the ones that wrapped around the brim of her nearly identical hat.

The hat is stuffed somewhere in this duffel, the one I haven't unpacked. I go piece by piece, taking out what I need. I haven't moved it from the hallway where it has been since the first night I got to New York, months ago.

I do a wash of clothing and sheets every now and then. Here things don't get dirty, not like there. Seated on the top of my duffle I braid and unbraid the ribbons. When I have done it enough times so I won't forget how the material feels between my fingers, I walk out of the apartment and take my hat to the end of the hallway and pull the metal handle toward me. The door to the chute is heavy. Now, after, I wish I had not pulled it open. My hat is gone. I threw it down and I am standing listening to the sound of it falling. It is made of hard felt and it bangs against the metal sides of the shaft for twenty floors.

CHAPTER 3

IT IS THE END of the day check-in before they let me
go home. The doctors know it is important that I am on time. I
worry when someone is late. Late might mean gone. It is why I
never make anyone wait.

Or else they are testing me to see if I lose my temper. It is
because of what I said today about the hat. I might have given
them reason to revoke my privileges of coming and going.

CHAPTER 4

KARL WROTE TO ME for many years after I left. His envelopes were blue. I remember some of his letters by heart. To remember by heart is to remember by feel. This is the worst way to remember.

I saved this one. I received it the day after I married Richard.

> *Lisette,*
> *I will be going to Lake Titicaca in a week, remember on the hammock we spoke of this. Maybe you will join me. I am only joking. The garden is doing well. You would be very pleased with the tomatoes although no one here likes tomatoes. They prefer apples. The greenhouse of plastic sheeting works. I only need to remember to water every day. Blanca will do it while I am gone.*
>
> *I am writing to you from the hammock at night. This means it is safer here. I am hopeful change is going to come. I have always said what we saw, which was the worst of it, could not go on.*
> *Love,*
> *Karl*

Then, I was filling in blanks on application forms. And when acceptances arrived I agreed to spend the next three years in a law school that looked like a toaster with a view of the overpass on Amsterdam Avenue.

The books that came with the toaster were maroon and navy and had simple names. A story in one called *Property* went this way:

A man and his neighbor argue over a tract of land called Blackacre. There is resolution and a rule to be applied the next time there is a disagreement.

The nightmares with the disembodied heads began.

At night I was surrounded by blood-streaked stalks of corn. The setting was like Blackacre described in my law books. But every place was Perú.

I walked across a podium.

A man in a robe that reached to the floor handed me my degree. It was wrapped in a cylinder and tied with black cord.

The dogs had hung from black cord. The man's gown was black. I tripped but caught myself. I made it back to my seat. To calm myself, I said you are home now, this is New York, you are safe. I gave the cord to the student next to me. He did not know why and I didn't know how to answer when he asked.

I put on a navy suit and white pressed shirt and black pumps. The office I went to had a door with a nameplate. It was my name. By the end of my first day, the starch in my shirt chafed my neck. But the noose had gone to Pablo. It could have also been true, but I didn't know for sure, that this was what they did to Enrique. And if not to Enrique exactly this way, then to all the other Pablos that had been hanged, along with and like the dogs—from trees, the eucalyptus and pine, even from the willows.

CHAPTER 5

I TELL THE DOCTOR about our last vacation. The way caravans of families surround us. I use my hands and draw a wide circle indicating the beach. Everyone knows, somehow, the acceptable distance for parking their four-wheel drive vehicles so as not to infringe on the next family's compound. It would be easy to mistake someone's husband for one's own. Our coolers, chairs and fancy umbrellas with German gears are all alike. We turn the sand plastic-colored.

Not noticing is vacation. Richard not noticing has always troubled me. Because of Perú I can never not notice. During the year I don't hear seagulls so when I am on vacation I want to hear them. At first I enjoy their mating calls but as the week goes on the sound becomes a cry that blocks out most everything, even the sound of the waves.

Before noon I have eaten lunch. There's a hungry sort of boredom to the beach. Weeks before I told Richard I wanted to go to Barcelona.

Ben said, and Phoebe agreed, anywhere but a desolate beach.

I was perfectly clear, Phoebe needed to be near people and Ben and I have never liked the sun.

But now Ben inflates the raft while Richard sits on a chair

positioned in alignment with the sun to tan most perfectly. His lit cigar points to the horizon.

When they were little I took them to the park. I keep on talking about this, even though it seems to me the doctor wants me to focus on Perú, to stay there until I have exorcised Perú, but I keep going. I should have let them play the way the other mothers did.

How's that? she asks.

They ignored their children. That way they were free to chatter with one another. I liked to have Ben and Phoebe look at any one thing and then, with their eyes shut, I asked them to tell me what they remembered.

Phoebe said, a yellow flower.

Ben disagreed, five thousand pin pricks attached to a slender thread.

Phoebe said, no, it's a green leaf.

Ben opened his eyes and insisted, interconnected veins with water rushing toward a center.

I said to him, your eyes are bright enough to illuminate the entire world.

That can't be true, the entire world is too large, Ben says. What I see are four swings lined in a row and the trees with their dresses of leaves.

I pointed to the shadows made by the oak tree. Look at the way the light filters through the leaves. It's the angle of the sun that determines where the shadows fall. The sun at the equator is always the same. This means the shadows don't change. If you remember from day to day, you can return and find your favorite shadow just where you left it.

Phoebe and Ben rolled their eyes and laughed.

I looked away, then back again. And this time when I saw them, they were older.

Ben said, I see beneath the children's dirt-streaked faces.

What else?

They're missing something. He looked at the ground and made a circle in the sand with the toe of his shoe. Mother, they need an answer.

To what?

That's the problem. They don't know the question, not yet. He bent down and picked up a clear pebble, smooth like sea glass, and rolled it in his palm. They want to know what life is.

The doctor lets me cry. I could keep going but she interrupts. What are you planning to prepare for dinner?

Is she trying to determine if I'm negligent?

Maybe she thinks I made these things up about Ben and Phoebe.

Really, I want to say, this is the way I remember it.

I say, steak.

Because I want to go home.

CHAPTER 6

AT THE NEXT SESSION the doctor asks how the steak was.

I stare at her neatly crossed legs.

She doesn't really want to know.

She picks a piece of lint from her woolen jacket.

It's her way of checking facts. I want to say, I'm the lawyer. Instead I say, fine, thank you.

There was no steak. We didn't get hungry until midnight and that's when we ate. We wanted popcorn so I brought it into bed with us.

Steak and French fries. Homemade, I say.

I should have stopped with the French fries. The more detailed, the more a lie sounds like a lie. I hope she'll think the lie was about the homemade fries. It's the steak part she needs to believe. No steak might result in a call to a social worker. A stout middle-aged woman will arrive to the house unannounced with pad and pencil. She will note what canned goods are on the shelves and what is in the garbage. This will lead to a series of questions because the pantry is stocked with just capers, popcorn and toilet paper.

·   ·   ·

Karl and I spent one weekend at a beach on the equator. It was after the rainy season. It wasn't until we floated naked in the ocean the first night—soothing our badly burned skin—that we realized how close we were to the sun. The full moon lit the tips of my breasts and Karl's toes as they pointed upward toward Orion's belt. At dawn we left the water and crawled beneath the mosquito netting. That's when he said he loved me. I was sure I was dreaming.

Why? the doctor asks.

Why what?

Why were you sure you were dreaming?

My mother left me in the hospital. The red on my face wouldn't look good in the family album. It was hard for her to look at me. I understand. I find it difficult too. But I don't want to talk about this. It's Richard, leaving Richard. That is what is on my mind. It was on my mind for at least five years. Before that beach vacation I tried but hadn't been able. It is why I am on that beach flicking dead bugs off the cover of *The Book of Illusions*. I walk away. Then I'm running and when I stop to catch my breath, I study the sand between my toes—black, red, brown and a shard of glass. I'm looking at the horizon because I have no one to talk to. Richard is smoking. The kids have had it with both of us. It's a family vacation where none of us feels much toward one another, except perhaps antipathy.

I hate that Richard smokes cigars. He knows this. I stop mentioning it to him because it doesn't make a difference. Even still, I try to sit back down next to him thinking maybe we'll talk, and I can't concentrate on reading. I have to keep repositioning my chair to avoid his fumes. When the breeze dies down I try again. But each time I find my place the wind shifts and the smoke from his cigar makes me cough.

Phoebe is sprawled across a yellow towel.

Ben is bored.

I ask if they want to go on the raft.

Reluctantly they agree.

Phoebe talks about the book she is reading. Ben does too, except his is on the Armenian genocide.

Virginia Woolf mentions that in *Mrs. Dalloway*, I say.

Phoebe scrunches her face into a wrinkle and holds her hand in front of her, Stop. I don't want to hear about it. This is my vacation, too.

Gulls swoop down but come up with nothing. The only fish are the decayed ones along the shore. The plastic oars cut through the water but I lose control of the circles I am making.

At the sandbar I pull the raft to higher ground. There are dead fish and the air smells of rot.

El Frontón. The smell of gull shit was everywhere outside that prison. We made it to the exit. As soon as the door was opened Karl took a very deep breath. He gagged and had difficulty catching his breath. I was sure he was going to vomit but he held it back.

Vultures and gulls were eating the dead things that bobbed on the surface of the water. We didn't let ourselves consider what might have been in there and not just floating, all the things that had sunk or had gotten caught between the rocks.

Human-sized shit is what I am seeing in our vacation ocean. And when the sun lights up the seaweed I see toes that are not connected to anything. I shake my head left and right, hard, and then again.

Phoebe wants to know what's wrong.

The sun, maybe I have sunstroke.

Really?

No, Phoebe, not really.

Phoebe collects broken shells.

I point to my sun-screened arm, ash from your father's cigar.

Ben pushes Phoebe and she is angry with him.

What do you expect, Phoebe, here at the beach? Besides, you wanted to come.

I did not.

Then you should have said no. If you had then maybe we wouldn't be here.

The boat swirls like toilet paper on the sides of a clogged toilet.

I am unable to break the pull of the two currents. My right arm is weaker than my left so we keep going in a circle. Sweat is beading on my upper lip. With my teeth clenched I am determined. Finally we are moving toward the shore.

The chair Richard is sitting on is a red dot getting larger.

I drag the boat close to the car so the incoming tide won't take it.

Richard looks up. Seems as if you had trouble, he says.

You could tell?

He nods yes.

How long would you have waited?

For what?

Until you realized I needed help.

You never need help.

CHAPTER 7

RICHARD HANDS ME a wrapped box. Anniversary day. This will be our last. We don't yet know this.

I have nothing for him. Inside his box is a wallet. I keep looking at it, hoping in the looking it will turn into something else. Or I will be able to make it disappear.

I open my eyes and it is still there.

Richard, too.

Is he saying, you are spent. Him too. Or could he be saying he owns me, he bought me when I said I do. When he said it too.

Sixteen years equals three wallets. This year's wallet is identical to the one he gave me five years ago. The one I returned. This time it means—I'm stuck with It, the It being him. That this It is following me.

I want to say, a wallet! But these words would have hung in the air like his smell.

A black wallet. Black is when there are no streetlights. Don't look into the ravine to the place beneath the *cabuye,* the cactus with the thorns, where they bashed his head with a stone.

And black is the corridor color of each prison we walked through. When blood is old and dried it is so black you cannot imagine it once ran red. The wallet five years ago was red. That is even worse than black.

You like to stash things in small places, he says.

I manage a smile, that's true. I do.

Now I feel awful. I go to my side of the bed and bury my head beneath the pillows. The ones that smell like him I toss to the floor. My tears are salty. Salt on split lips stings.

The doctor rarely moves. Not even to place behind her ear that one wisp of hair, that disobedient strand, or to wake up a crossed and now sleeping leg. It can't be true that her legs don't go to sleep.

The dream probably was because of the wallet—I say loudly.

She grimaces.

A wallet has to do with buying food. With feeding a family. In the dream, he's accusing me of not being able to take care of them.

She uncrosses her legs. The bottoms of her shoes aren't worn. She floats wherever she goes.

CHAPTER 8

NO LEAK IN THE CEILING.

It hasn't rained for a very long time. Even if it had, only the penthouse would leak and we don't live on the top floor. The lintel could be rotted though. That would be a way to get rain. But to date our lintels have never leaked even with directed wind.

Ben and Phoebe are still sleeping. Outside the bedroom window, if I crane my neck to see, the grass is wheat-colored, so dry it crunches.

Richard is in the kitchen. Where he always is on a Sunday. I make the trek of thirteen steps to the foyer and then seven more to the kitchen. He knows I need coffee but begins to tell me how much I've hurt Ben. Now that he has started he isn't able to calm down. I hope he's wrong about me not committing, about how I let Ben vacillate from this to that. I think that's what he's saying.

Lisette, what are you teaching them?

I think but don't say, not to sit still when they are uncomfortable. Or when something isn't right. To know there are options. I don't want them to be victims, not to things they can change.

I pour a glass of juice. I can see it landing in the middle of his forehead. But children should not wake to the sound of shattering glass. Not glass their mother throws at their father.

Richard is still seated at the kitchen table. I say, it is time for you to leave. But saying it doesn't bring relief, not like I thought it would.

The silence that rests on us is the kind that precedes something dreadful. When I begin to speak my voice is not familiar. It's how you treat Ben, I say. It's how we treat each other.

Then I run my fingers across my corduroy pants. The lines in the grain of the floor dead-end into a seam clogged with dirt from all the people and pets that have walked here. I like the shiny parts. Also the splintered ones. There is one special place in the corner where a whole chunk of wood is missing.

Things happen, Richard says.

Is Ben a part of these 'things'? I need to protect Ben.

He walks toward me.

I get up and back away.

What did you just say?

For you Ben is trouble. He challenges you but worse he reminds you of me. You think he is defying you but I'm the one with the will you so dislike.

He fills a glass with water.

I ask for one too.

He hands me his. But before I have it firmly in my hand, he lets go. We watch it fall and shatter.

In the bedroom he is slamming the dresser drawers.

I go outside to the terrace. My terra-cotta planters are crammed with dead herbs. If I need to, I can jump the three floors and be safe. This must be what Karl and Richard meant when they said I think like a child.

My hammock is strung across a metal frame. I still sleep in it sometimes. In spring, after the thawing and freezing of winter, many cement chunks from the foundation have come undone, crushing the sprouting crocuses and daffodils below. Nothing is heavy enough to damage the rhododendron bushes.

From my hammock I can see Phoebe and Ben's clubhouse. It is built into the corner of the building. Richard did that when they were little, when their toys and strollers and car seats took up too much space. It wasn't until they were older that they turned it into a clubhouse. Ben's fire-dog pajamas are still draped across the front window; Phoebe's poodle-dog pajamas are stretched along the side. The first thing hanging above the doorway is a bicycle.

Not like the ones we owned in the Andes.

What would have happened if one thing had been different?

Next come the discarded plastic toys. Stacked on the shelves is an old radio with knobs, a telephone, the kind you can dial, and in the child-size desk pressed leaves are ironed between wax paper. The clubhouse is also where they kept different colored ink pads and pictures on rubber stamps. The smaller treasures, including shells from the beach, are wrapped in pieces of tissue.

Even when it is freezing, if I'm on my hammock looking at their clubhouse, I am able to fall into a peaceful sleep.

Above the *cuyera* between the two eucalyptus trees Karl would read to me using his flashlight, or, if we had forgotten, he would recite César Vallejo from memory,

> *Algo te identifica con el que se aleja de ti, y es la facultad*
> *común de volver: de ahí tu más grande pesadumbre.*
> *Algo te separa del que se queda contigo, y es la esclavitud*
> *común de partir: de ahí tus más nimios regocijos.*

Something identifies you with the one who leaves you,
    and it is your common power to return: thus your
    greatest sorrow.
Something separates you from the one who remains
    with you, and it is your common slavery to depart:
    thus your meagerest rejoicing.

Here in the cold New York winter I am able to close my eyes and bring him to me as I fall asleep, floating in my hammock. And if he comes I hold onto him until morning. What wakes me is the way the cold air hurts as it settles in my lungs.

As I am awakening I turn and reach my hand out and run my fingertips across the tops of the bushes. These are the bushes I will hack to the ground in spring even though they are not dead.

CHAPTER 9

NO, I'D RATHER NOT, I say.

Why is that?

It's just a place.

The doctor tries to get me to look her in the eye.

The rhododendron bushes. The missing. I'm always seeing what's missing. Lucana . . .

I'm looking at the trees. Wondering why the leaves have to die each winter. I say, marca, then machetes.

What?

I don't have to answer.

In Luca . . . , she says, I'm sorry I didn't catch the name of the place.

There wasn't anything left, I say quickly.

She looks at me.

It was after. I'm impatient. We came after. I don't think anyone was able to get inside before it was all gone. I never heard an accounting made by an outsider, you know, an investigator or some trained professional who might have carefully reconstructed what happened. All I heard was what the villagers said or what *Sendero* said and that sounded like bragging. We got there and really, I don't remember much. In fact, there was nothing to see.

[108]

What do you mean, nothing?

They were hit from both sides. The rebels came first. Then the military. Then nothing.

FROM OUR BEDROOM window I could see the Andes, and closer still, our outdoor spigot. Once the water came out the color of rust.

When the clouds lifted, after six months of rain, it looked as if the summit could be reached in an afternoon. On the full moon the old woman in charge of spirits stood before its snow-capped face howling to the men buried in an avalanche of prehistoric ice. We were told never to interrupt her, not until she had finished reciting every last name.

Karl's brother came at the end of the rainy season. I have photographs of them scaling glacial ice, using picks and crampons. They made it to the top.

The day they came down I prepared a feast. I tied the chicken's talons with string, severed the head with a cleaver using the flat stone in the backyard as the killing block. The killing always made me dizzy. This time the blood spurted up. I looked at my shirt to see if it was stained. A drop of blood dribbled down my forehead. From the corner of my eye I could see the thing still wiggling. I sat on the mud and put my head between my legs.

Karl, I called in the direction of the house.

His brother came.

After I drank four glasses of wine I asked Karl to come outside. We stood behind the house and looked at the mountain
Karl and his brother had just climbed. I couldn't get the words
out. In my pocket was the piece of paper from the lab. I handed
it to him. He knew the word for pregnant: *embarazada*.

Two days later I left for Washington.

It was Easter. I carried a round-trip ticket in my bag. In the
part that zippered I had a photograph of Karl standing at the
edge of the salt fields. He cupped salt in one hand as he poured
it through the fingers of the other. It is something he knows
how to do, harvest salt.

I reached inside my bag for the yogurt and used a tiny spoon
to bring it to my mouth, hoping it would settle my stomach.

I had been to Washington before. A friend and I stopped for
the night at a motel outside the city. We heard a woman scream
in the parking lot. We saw the shadow of a man holding her
back by her hair. It looked as if her neck might snap. Then
he pushed her away, taking the purse she had been holding
tightly against her chest before he ran into the alley.

This time I spent the first hour in my hotel room staring at
the stream of traffic, eating candy and drinking soda from the
mini bar. The American doctor in Lima had given me a list. I
dialed the first number. What I was arranging was illegal in
Perú. In Washington it was easy, next morning, first thing.

I didn't shower. I didn't care if I smelled badly and I didn't
want to wake up. Other women were waiting. I didn't look up
until I needed to use the bathroom and even then I walked
with my head tucked into my chest.

During the procedure the nurse held my hand and when
I pulled it away to cover my eyes, my palm was wet and
slippery.

There were papers to sign at the beginning and at the end. When I left she gave me nothing. I was expecting something. I wanted to know the sex and if not the sex then any one detail. But there were none.

I'm alone now, I wrote in the telegram. As I formed the last letter I tasted salt. It began to fill my mouth. I had trouble catching my breath. The telegraph operator offered me a cup of water.

Sometimes my child comes to me and asks, do I have a name?

No. No name.

CHAPTER 11

PHOEBE CAME into my bed, sunk her head into my abdomen, the bones of her skull pressed against my spine. Once she lived inside me. The beating of my heart is more familiar to her than it is to me. I cannot bundle her small and return her and even if I could she would refuse.

Part V

CHAPTER 1

I SCRAPE MY PALMS against the bottom of the pool. I focus on the moving shapes and shadows, they are like continents on the map I am charting in my mind of a place I have never been. When I arrive I will be given a different name. I will not be born ugly and this time, mother will not refuse me.

From the pool to the shower to the car. Each strand of hair is encased in ice. It would take just one of these iced daggers to pierce that major artery in my neck.

I am falling for a very long time before the pavement rises to catch me. The black icy surface is getting closer and I do not want it to touch me. It will be cold and hard. But there is nothing that can be done to stop from landing. Before the wheels touch the runway, a plane cannot change its course and soar.

CHAPTER **2**

THE PHONE RINGS. This hardly ever happens. I'm awake and then asleep until the next ring. It stops. I could go on this way not feeling thirst or hunger. Today, however, Phoebe is relying on me to get her up. Ben no longer does.

The shower drain is off center.

Phoebe demands a centered part.

I can't find it. If I ever do I will draw a line down the middle of her scalp with permanent marker.

The shower water runs down the pipes, taking with it hair and dead skin. These things run beneath the bathroom floor, along the kitchen wall, across the basement ceiling and out the waste drain attached to the laundry room sink.

Phoebe, we're late.

I need a day off.

What do you want for breakfast?

I'm not going.

Where's your project?

It's a Valentine's box. I drew hearts on tin foil with red magic marker. It can't get wet.

I'll wrap it in plastic. Let's go.

Why?

I have work and you have school.

Why?

It's what we do.

The music teacher opens the car door with one hand and holds an umbrella in the other. Phoebe slides across the back seat, kicking the bag into the gutter which is now a stream of rushing water. Phoebe bends down and brings the dripping Valentine's box to safety. As she is wiping the hair and rain from her eyes, I see red magic marker smeared across her cheek. This is what I must have looked like as a child. We have the same face. She is trembling but walks inside with the teacher. The last thing I see is the red hem of her skirt. This is when I know I am not going to be able to pull myself to work.

From the side of the road I call the doctor. She gives me an address. The first person I see is an old man with a walking stick. I ask for directions. But I have to interrupt to see if he could write the street names out, maybe draw a rudimentary map. I don't tell him I have forgotten where the spaces between the words go.

I order the mess inside my car before I drive away. If they see it this way they might keep me longer. Half-empty bottles of water, pieces of chewed gum in shreds of bottle labels and on the passenger side seat last week's *New York Times* unopened and a stack of library books long overdue.

CHAPTER 3

I DON'T WANT TO BE HERE.

Why? The doctor asks.

I don't want to be falling apart.

Are you?

I decide not to look up. Is there a pill to take to avoid the next stretch? The part where I collapse? If I can sleep I dream of not being able to do what I'm supposed to do.

My sister is with me in my old apartment. She has a cat and it's in the way because I need her help. I ask her to put the cat down. She says it will go to an open window and drop eleven floors, that the apartment is an inferno.

Instinct is knowing when not to jump. Cats know that sort of thing, I say. It is babies you have to worry about. Instinct is an inferior state in that it implies reflex, not thought. The thought part is what separates us from the cat.

If the windows had screens or I had air conditioning she would have some other reason.

Why are so many people here?

My sister looks concerned, as if she knows what's happening to me. We were once friends.

Do you have an ashtray?

Use the floor. There isn't enough food and if I run to the market, the chicken will burn.

That doesn't look like chicken.

It's veal. The sink is fine for your ashes, and veal burns like chicken.

I don't have anything green. I ask for a cigarette. There are food scraps everywhere. I stick my head in the refrigerator, put cubes of ice down my bra and press two more against the back of my neck. The room goes blurry. I stare at the refrigerator door. Slowly my vision is restored but what I'm seeing isn't there. It is the shopping list Karl wrote twenty years ago. Clementines, quinoa, orange juice.

I'm sure my sister has left because I hear the front door open and then her kind of slam. The walls begin to merge. Instinct tells me to fight them.

My grandfather says, she's sick, she needs to go to the hospital. He blows his nose. I turn icy. I am the only she.

I look at the floor. Take my shoes off. Mostly to stall. I'm not sure the stalling will work in which case I will have to go. Better to go with two shoes on and putting one on is easier than two. This must be why I only take one off. The left one.

To calm myself I rub between my toes. When we came down from Machu Picchu Karl gave me an apple from his knapsack. Then he took off my hiking boots and rubbed my feet.

I want my grandfather to stop crying. I try to think of something to say that will cheer him up. I hate hospitals. With one shoe on and one off, the floor is even. I'm at the oven with my mitt, the one with the cows jumping over the moon. I peer past the greasy window. Had I cleaned it, I would be able to see the burned veal without having to open the door, without allowing all the heat to escape.

I don't have enough food. There are more people than I expected.

My grandmother says, that was always the number, twelve.

Someone should go to the store. No one volunteers so I apologize, just an idea.

I need to make my grandfather stop crying. All I can think of is if I can show him the yogurt and cheese he'll see I have something to eat. But that's when the refrigerator collapses. The sides just give way.

I pick my arms up from my lap and bring them to my chin, then clasp them together and let them drop back into my lap where they fold into themselves, like a house of cards.

CHAPTER 4

I TELL THE DOCTOR about the house falling apart, that I don't think I can keep it up much longer.

Keep what up?

The idea of having to go back to work. There's a kind of lizard in the Amazon with poisonous saliva. If a drop gets on its prey, the poison immobilizes the thing, so even if it is ten times the size of the lizard, the prey is unable to move, giving the lizard time to kill and eat it. Work is that poisonous drop.

I look away.

Snow is falling. Snow globes are not real. The cinderblock walls are. I reach for a Kleenex. This could be a TB hospital in the countryside at the turn of the last century. I wish the doctor would go away.

Nonsense, she interrupts.

Being a lawyer never made sense, except as a way to escape the chaos. It makes even less sense now. Am I losing ground?

No. You said it never made sense.

The fire alarm rings. I jump from my seat and rush to the door. The doctor is still sitting, looking me up and down.

Aren't you going to leave the building?

No, she says.

No? I think she's fucking crazy. She must have seen this in my expression.

Let's wait a minute. It's probably a false alarm. It happens a lot. Often it is the wiring. Especially when it rains.

But it isn't raining. I got up so quickly the chair tipped. I'd rather wait outside.

You would?

I'm annoyed and panicked. Does everything have to be a bloody psychological exam! When an alarm sounds I take it seriously. That's what you're supposed to do. It's what the fire department is relying on you to do. They want us to run, it is less work for them.

She picks up the phone and calls the office, then motions for me to sit, only a patient, she says.

Just a patient? A patient on fire!

A patient was tampering with the alarm. The fire department will have to come regardless. When you hear the sirens, relax. It's the law, they have to show up and make sure everything is in order. We were saying the practice of law never made much sense.

It's worse now. When I'm at the door that leads into the law firm I start sweating. It's habit that gets me from the house to that elevator. Once inside I'll be gripped with dread as I hang my coat. It is as if I'm sacrificing myself.

That's an odd word.

What?

Sacrificing.

I said that?

You said 'sacrificing.'

I'm looking at her patent leather shoe. Not at all scuffed. There's a funny scallop running around the opening. I wonder if it ever snags her stockings and makes them run. Her foot size is about the same as mine.

What does it make you think of?

There is a story I heard in Perú. An Indian told it over *chicha*. But he wasn't drunk.

The man who sees God arrives into town on foot. It isn't clear where he comes from but his clothes are worn and dust-covered. He's been walking a long time. A wineskin hangs from his right shoulder. When he checks into the hotel overlooking the square, he insists on a room facing the church, the one where worshippers buy thin sheets of gold to rub into the altar. He's never been inside and it isn't church he wants but a very cold beer and a woman in see-through red silk. She will just appear. He won't have to search or seduce her and if she comes he will keep God waiting.

He closes the door and jams the metal chair underneath the knob, not needing towels or any other thing. The photograph of his daughter is in his shirt pocket. In it she's laughing.

From the edge of the bed he studies the room. Through the foam mattress he feels the wooden frame. Hanging above the bed is a cross made of dried corn husks. A rag mat lies on the floor, worn to the warp, covering half a stain that looks like wine or blood, or something else that ran red. This mark of blood follows him. After opening the window he stares out. His eyes are parched from the dirt and dry air and he isn't feeling right.

A hot wind blows through the room. The sky is cloudless. It's siesta time and mostly quiet. A boy in long pants and rubber boots plays with a black ball while his three-legged dog watches.

He pushes his thinning hair back and draws a deep breath.

When he was walking it was God who told him to take this room that overlooks the *zocalo*. He isn't religious, doesn't even like the smell of incense, but it's that time of year: *el aniversario*.

His hair sticks to his neck and cheeks and his fingers are soiled. He's flushed and his face is sunburned and lined with road dust. There is a pitcher of water and an empty bowl. Once washed he goes outside. After crossing the square, he follows the path to the steps of the church. Inside there is an underground kind of damp. Overcome with fatigue he sleeps.

When he awakes an Indian is sitting next to him. The man knows it is God. God tells him to travel to an ancient Inca site. There he will be asked to make a sacrifice. Not until the blood saturates the killing stone and pools along the ground will the earth release his daughter.

He leaves the church at dusk and checks out of the hotel. Facing east he begins to walk. In the darkness he moves faster. The way is set before him as if he remembers it, but it can't be so because it is only in his sleep, or when half-crazed by loss, that he has tried to reach her. This time he knows where he is going, exactly.

When he arrives he finds nothing but a shred of bright clothing.

Either his daughter has been eaten by wild animals, bones and skull and all, or the ground has opened and swallowed her whole.

What does the story mean to you? the doctor asks.

The desire to bring back the dead.

What's dead?

I blow my nose. I look the doctor in the eye. So many of them. And in a way Arye and Karl too.

What about the father looking for his lost daughter?

What about it?

What does that mean to you?

That part, I inhale deeply as if it is my last chance to find air. That is the part that never happened.

CHAPTER 5

WHAT DID YOU BRING? The doctor asks.

The box is on my lap.

Photographs of Perú.

I take a deep breath and open it. This is Arye from the first time I went to Perú. I didn't think I would go back, not after what I had seen. I caught him in the corner of the frame. The picture is a scorched field.

This was twenty-five years ago. Here's a page from my journal.

> *Freezing cold. I left my hat in the hotel. We drive for more than three hours then hike another two. A man who identifies himself as Manuel talks to Pablo in Quechua. This is where they took me, he says as he nervously kicks the dust on the floor.*
>
> *It hasn't rained for weeks. Rolff can't wear his contact lenses because of the dust. We are standing in a shell of what was once a building. The roof is missing and the walls, made of adobe, are crumbling. There are many interconnected rooms.*

You see, Manuel points, these holes in the wall are where the shackles were mounted. They locked me to them with my hands above my head. I hung that way at least a night and a day because I remember the sun setting and rising. They put a stool under my legs but I could barely reach it.

I kept going in and out of consciousness. They threw buckets of freezing cold water on me.

I heard my brother in another room. They were torturing him. I wasn't sure it was Jorge. But they kept telling me it was. I couldn't stop asking. Then they would tell me another detail about him. I don't know for sure if it was my brother. But when they let me go they told me Jorge had been taken back to the village. It wasn't true. When I got home he was not there. There were no more houses and the animals were gone. No one was left. I never found my brother. I don't know if that was his voice I kept hearing. It is the voice I still hear. It wakes me up at night, it won't stop.

Arye began questioning Manuel about his brother, asking things like when was the last time you saw him, how old was he, was he living with your parents at the time. Maybe Arye was trying to be helpful. But by then he had to have known how unlikely it would have been, finding Jorge. There was no reason to question Manuel that way. Arye should have known, that this was the time, the time to cry.

Part VI

CHAPTER 1

THE HUDSON RIVER laps against the landfill of lower Manhattan, stretches to the bedrock of New Jersey. Outlines of tree branches reflect like jagged spears. I have been walking for a long time.

I come most every day. It is a secret, this walk. I'm in Perú but I am afraid to tell Phoebe and Ben. It is more than thinking of Perú. I allow Perú to enter me. I am being summoned.

I can look at the photographs now even though there was a time I wanted to burn them. I have had enough burning.

Last night I went through another box and found a statue of the Virgin Mary. It is the one I bought in a shantytown outside of Lima, with eyes that see. Not dead eyes like the others. The woman who owned the store knew the difference.

There is also incense. She sold me labdanum and myrrh. Labdanum is extracted from the roses that grow between the rocks above the shoreline. They bloom infrequently and often die before being seen. I used to read this poem by Cesar Vallejo. This page is in here because I had carried it with me so I could memorize it. I don't think I can recite it from memory any longer.

Los Nueve Monstruos

Pues de resultas
del dolor, hay algunos
que nacen, otros crecen, otros mueren,
y otros que nacen y no mueren, otros
que sin haber nacido, mueren, y otros
que no nacen ni mueren (Son los más).
Y también de resultas
del sufrimiento, estoy triste
hasta la cabeza, y más triste hasta el tobillo,
de ver al pan, crucificado, al nabo,
ensangrentado,
llorando, a la cebolla,
al cereal, en general, harina,
a la sal, hecha polvo, el agua, huyendo.

The Nine Monsters

For as a result
of the pain, there are some
who are born, others grow, others die,
and others who are born and do not die, others
who without having been born, die, and others
who neither are born nor die (The most).
And also as a result
of suffering, I am sad
up to my head, and sadder down to my ankle,
from seeing bread, crucified, the turnip,
bloodied,
the onion, crying,
cereal, in general, flour,
salt, ground to dust, water fleeing.

CHAPTER 2

KARL STAYED in our village for many years after I left. This letter is from five years later. I was married, I think he knew but I'm not sure, maybe not.

> *Dear Lisette,*
>
> *It is safer now. Something happened yesterday I think you should know. I want to tell you even though I don't expect you will come back. But what happened last night should bring you some peace that those who have survived may be able to go about their lives less frightened. There is a sense of order returning. Nothing monumental. Perú has learned there is no such thing as monumental change, not even with the most extreme violence. What I mean is maybe it will be better than it was during the years of violence. It pains me to think that after all this agony we are not yet back to the place before it started.*
>
> *Amparo never gave up looking for Enrique. Last night three men came to the village and asked to speak with her. The men said they had seen Enrique being murdered. They are Senderistas. They were encamped fifteen miles north of here almost exactly in the area where we speculated the military had been. That night the Senderistas separated into*

two groups because they knew the military was closing in. One group stayed behind at the camp and was wiped out. The other walked down the mountain. The man who took us last night said Enrique was hooded and tied up in the back of a pickup truck. He recognized him not just because he was head of the cabildo but because he knew his voice. He said Enrique was well respected. The military made the prisoners get out and stand in the ravine that runs parallel to the Pan American. It was late. That is where they killed them, on the side of the road.

The men argued it wasn't safe to leave the bodies even if they buried them. Maybe they were lazy or scared but they decided not to move them. They buried them right where they had fallen.

They came because they knew Amparo was still looking. They couldn't come before because it wasn't safe.

And in the grave, right where they remembered, we found a piece of his poncho, the one he was wearing that night. The red one. We found the rest of him. We will bury him in the apple orchard. The one you and I helped to plant. I think you should know this even though I do not understand what has happened to you. Why it is that you do not want to know.

It is the knowing that will free you.

Blanca asks about you. I told her we are no longer in touch. Then she asked if you were dead. If you want you can write to her through me.

Karlos

CHAPTER 3

THE TRUTH and Reconciliation Commission was convened.

Karlos wrote requesting my negatives. I sent everything.

It is possible Arye was the forensic anthropologist working in our area. And it is possible that Arye touched a bone that belonged to Cholo or Lobo or someone else we once knew.

Karl has a daughter now, younger than the one we would have had. I know this because he told me face to face.

I see you.

Karl.

Karlos.

You are the last one to pass through immigration and for a few minutes I think maybe you changed your mind. That you did not come. It has been two decades. We see each other across the room, stare, then look away.

We finish a bottle of red wine. You need to walk. On the street you point to a man. But our dead friend, this man we both see to be Enrique, doesn't turn around, doesn't recognize us, and so we let him keep on walking. He passes through an opening into Riverside Park and is swallowed by the night, by what looms on the other side of the darkened tree trunks.

Every now and then the clouds move and a half-crescent moon lights the way. But the stars never seem as far as they really are.

The red wine in last night's glass reminds me of the hand of the man who wanted to shake mine. Instinctively I knew not to take it, even though he had come from the same opera and was eating in the same restaurant. There is blood everywhere. It follows you. I saw enough to say for sure his fingernails were trimmed and filed smooth with not one rough edge. You were always a person or two or three away from a blood-stained hand. Even after traveling nine hours north by plane.

There are days and nights when wine doesn't work, nor sleep, or the persistence of the mountains. Then come the dark days when it isn't worth trying.

You will always be in the mountains. This is where I would look for you, if I ever look for you, bundled and sealed against the weather. You will be in a coat and it will be raining.

Nine o'clock at night. The fish you bought for dinner is still wrapped in paper. You forgot to put it in the refrigerator and the ice that once protected it from spoiling has melted. Now the bloated bundle sits in a shallow puddle on a blue plate.

They pulled all those distended bodies from the rivers. The military went through a lot of trouble, dumping them from helicopters with weights tied to their ankles, men at desks plotting the way the corpses were to fall.

      ·   ·   ·

In *The Tin Drum* the mother throws buckets of fish down the cellar stairs. The squirming half-live prehistoric bodies bury her small son standing wide-eyed at the bottom. The world beyond their locked door is in chaos, men gone mad. The boy closes his eyes and stands perfectly still.

Does fish taste different if it is eaten close to where it is harvested? Here in the northern hemisphere they tell us not to buy it, that it is over-fished or poisonous. When you look out at the sea you cannot tell they are nearly extinct and full of mercury. Even if you let yourself stare deep into the water, past the lapping waves, there are no clues. This is true of the mountains as well. What is missing cannot be seen.

This time we said a formal good-bye on the curb at Kennedy airport. There was rain falling from a dark and starless sky. I pulled away and in the rearview mirror watched as you got smaller. I couldn't tell if you turned around, if you were watching me leave. Your coat blended with the color of wet pavement. Then the details were gone.

CHAPTER 4

YOU SEND ME photographs of your Andes. The ones that are outside your bedroom window. These photographs remind me of the mountains we once saw together.

There was that time we lay in bed. The dog outside did not stop barking. I threw a tomato from the window to make him change his mind. He did not stop. The tomato never reached him. It hit the frame and splattered inside the room.

Like your face, you said.

We had knickers made from wool, one pair for you and one pair for me.

It turned out they were too warm.

When we were climbing we had to take them off and continue in our underwear and hiking boots. There is a photograph of us this way. I set the camera on an outcropping of rock and when it was doing the countdown of thirty seconds—we saw how long thirty seconds really is—I ran back and stood underneath the crook of your arm. Only the camera and the condors saw us this way.

· · ·

When we were at Machu Picchu no one else was there. *Sendero* kept everyone away. A storm sent us in search of a dry place and underneath a stone outcropping, perhaps an ancient altar of what was once a temple, we sat and listened to the rain.

You said, there are temples and living quarters at Machu Picchu for women only.

We drank wine from your wineskin.

This must be one of those temples. This altar is where the Inca made their sacrifices. Lay me out across the cold hard stone and do what must be done. The stain on my face is why I am here.

We watched the rain hit the perfectly flat stones. When the wine was gone, I said, I want more.

You gave me your wine-stained tongue.

And I gave you mine.

The ground was soft with silt like dust.

You pulled me on top of you. Our clothes were off. And it was warm. I reached my hand outside the stone awning and brought the rain back to you. You licked my hand. And when you were done, I cupped some more but you pushed my hand aside and pinned me to the ground. The earth gave way. And as it did, you said, if we can have each other this way the losses will recede.

Stop talking, I said.

One last thing, you said, as you went deep inside me, this earth is fertile.

ACKNOWLEDGMENTS

I am most grateful to the gentle people of Gatazo Zambrano, Chimborazo Province, Ecuador. Especially the family Rea Cuvi and the young girl I once knew there (*a ti un abrazo fuerte*). On this side of the equator I wish to thank Sylvia Karasu and Harvey Klein for watching over me; my teacher, Terese Svoboda, a most gifted writer and tireless reader; Noy Holland for reminding me of the unspoken bonds between the living; and to all the many who gave me back my son, but especially the one who came the day before Thanksgiving bearing rocks, Oliver Sacks.

And to the three people who keep me moored to this earth: Andrew, Barnett, and Franny Koven.

LYNN LURIE, a resident of New York City, is an attorney with a Masters in International Affairs and a Masters in Fine Arts. She is a graduate of Barnard College and Columbia University. Lurie served as a Peace Corps volunteer in Ecuador (1980–82), during which time she procured funding from the U.S. Agency for International Development to build a factory in the highlands. On return to the United States she covered Ecuador, Panama, and Colombia for *Business International,* primarily as a financial reporter. She currently volunteers as a translator and administrator on medical trips to South America which provide surgery free of charge to indigent children. As an attorney Lurie has worked in Newark, N.J., at a community development corporation providing low income Section 8 housing under the Clinton administration. She has worked in the private sector, among other things on an initiative to repatriate Indian lands in the State of New Jersey to the Delaware Indians and in commercial transactions.

THE
JUNIPER
PRIZE

This volume is the third recipient of the Juniper Prize for Fiction, established in 2004 by the University of Massachusetts Press in collaboration with the UMass Amherst MFA Program for Poets and Writers, to be presented annually for an outstanding work of literary fiction. Like its sister award, the Juniper Prize for Poetry established in 1976, the prize is named in honor of Robert Francis (1901–1987), who lived for many years at Fort Juniper, Amherst, Massachusetts.